"Why you poor deluded gophers! You ain't dealin' with no danged story-book-hero—you're dealing with me, Smilin' Smith. I'm as peaceful a gent as you'll find in a ten days' ride—when I'm let alone. But let a gent step heavy on my toes an' I'm a ragin' fury, if I do say it as shouldn't.

"Smilin' Smith," he went on before the others could interrupt, "is a man what's always prided himself on bein' human, an' bein' such, is some susceptible to human impulses—good an' bad. Shucks, I wouldn't give two busted sticks for a gent what won't stand up for his rights. I like a feller what's human enough to cuss, chew, smoke an' drink. I do all them things myself. An' what's more, I got a good pair of fists an' I ain't a mite backward about usin' 'em!"

"Wind!" jeered Bast. "Nothin' but wind. If hot air was dollars, pilgrim, you'd be a sure-enough millionaire!"

"Yeah?"

As Smiling Smith jerked out the question, three swift strides brought him within a foot of the sneering Bast. Before the burly cattleman could guess his intention, the stranger's open palm smacked twice against the other's black-stubbled face—hard.

THE NO-GUN FIGHTER

NELSON NYE

CHARTER BOOKS, NEW YORK

THE NO-GUN FIGHTER

A Charter Book / published by arrangement with
the author

PRINTING HISTORY
Fourth printing / March 1984
Fifth printing / December 1985

ISBN: 0-441-58378-4

Charter Books are published by The Berkley Publishing Group,
200 Madison Avenue, New York, New York 10016.
PRINTED IN THE UNITED STATES OF AMERICA

CHAPTER 1

"YOU CAN'T GET AWAY WITH IT!"

"IT'S HECK, I reckon, but there's no gettin' around it." Banker Si Jones' mouth was grim. "That danged gunless jasper that rode in the other day on that flea-bitten crowbait has got an air-tight bill of sale for the Smithers' place."

A flat ominous silence descended on the room marked PRIVATE OFFICE in the Cowman's Bank of Bucksnort. Three important ranchers scowled at Banker Jones.

"Where in blazes did he pop up after us usin' that range for the last five years?" Jud Dixon queried savagely.

"Who cares?" growled "Two-Word" Brux. "He's here!"

"And right determined to roost," Si Jones complained with a bitter grimace.

"Seems tuh me," Al Bast remarked, "that we better try the discouragement method on him."

"Huh! You ain't seen him, Al." With skinny hands, the banker busied himself cutting slender strips from his desk blotter with a penknife. His sharp little eyes were screened by lowered lids. "He ain't to be taken lightly, I'll guarantee."

"He's got a jaw," added Dixon thoughtfully, "that's big and hard enough to block the Grand Canyon."

"Mean eye," Brux chipped in. "And fists—gosh durn!"

"Oh damn!" snapped Bast. "You old women give me a pain! There's ways of gettin' rid of him—the tougher they come, the harder they fall. If you gents is scared to get your paws dirty, leave him to me. I'll stop his clock. I've tamed stubborn coots before . . . . Haul out that bottle, Jones. I'm gettin' dry."

5

Abruptly, with no least regard for either the sanctity of private property or the sign on the frosted glass, the office door was flung open. Four heads jerked round as though pulled by a single string. Four pairs of eyes blinked incredulously at the man who grinned at them from the doorway, arms akimbo.

He was tall and hard and thin as a rail. His eyes, a frosty blue, leered impudently. Beneath his long Roman nose his lips were parted in a sardonic curve as he stood surveying the four astonished plotters.

"My, my!" he beamed with a chuckle. "Cat got your tongues, gents?"

"The gunless jasper!" Si Jones let out a high falsetto squeak.

The man in the doorway swept off his broad-brimmed sombero with an extravagant flourish. "Right as usual, Mister Jones." His grin widened. "How happy we all look—like a hawse with a burr under the saddle-blanket!"

"Your business?" demanded Brux, almost aggressively.

The stranger suddenly sobered, and as his facetiousness departed, his cold blue eyes gleamed distinctly hostile.

"Gents," he said, in his slow, hateful drawl, "when I showed Banker Jones my bill o' sale for the Smithers place, I sorta figgered to be let alone. Seems like I was a bit mistaken. Here's the four o' you yelpin' for my hide like a pack of mangy lobos."

"You been listenin' at the keyhole!"

"Correct again, Mister Jones."

"Eavesdroppin'!" Jud Dixon exploded.

"I shore have," the stranger admitted coolly. "Why you poor deluded gophers! You ain't dealin' with no danged story-book-hero—you're dealing with *me*, Smilin' Smith. I'm as peaceful a gent as you'll find in a ten-days' ride—when I'm let alone. But let a gent step heavy on my toes an' I'm a ragin' fury, if I do say it as shouldn't.

"Smilin' Smith," he went on before the others could interrupt, "is a man what's always prided himself on bein'

6

human, an' bein' such, is some susceptible to human impulses—good an' bad. Shucks, I wouldn't give two busted sticks for a gent what won't stand up for his rights. I like a feller what's human enough to cuss, chew, smoke an' drink. I do all them things myself. An' what's more, I got a good pair of fists an' I ain't a mite backward about usin' 'em!"

"Wind!" jeered Bast. "Nothin' but wind. If hot air was dollars, pilgrim, you'd be a sure-enough millionaire!"

"Yeah?"

As Smiling Smith jerked out the question, three swift strides brought him within a foot of the sneering Bast. Before the burly cattleman could guess his intention, the stranger's open palm smacked twice against the other's black-stubbled face—hard.

Features livid, Bast's hand swept downward for his gun. But even as his fingers spread to curl about its grip, his wrist was clamped by a vise-like hand. Slowly, inexorably, the rancher's wrist was twisted backward, in a hammerlock. With his free hand Smith calmly removed the tempting gun from the rancher's holster and threw it across the room.

"An' I hope it's busted to hell," he said as he released his hold and stepped back. "Gun's is one of the devil's inventions put on earth for the destruction of man. Now, what was it yuh said about wind?"

"Why, you—!" Bast spluttered.

"Ugh!" the grunt was wrung from the burly cattleman as Smith landed a heavy-handed smash to the jaw that toppled Bast backward, chair and all, sent him sprawling on the floor in an ignominious heap. And even as the burly rancher fell, Smith whirled like a startled cat and launched two lightning jolts which caught Jud Dixon, scrambling from his chair, full on the mouth. Blood spurted with the sound of snapping teeth. Jud Dixon, lips split and bleeding, went down for the count.

The Smiler rubbed his knuckles gently as he grinned at

Jones and Brux, who were staring in shocked amazement.

"I hope you gents will pardon me, if I seem a trifle rough," he drawled, and bowed his mocking bow.

"Gee-hossifer!" Brux drew a long breath. "What fists!"

Jones' beady eyes flickered, but his gimlet mouth remained closed.

"I reckon they asked for it, gents. But what's your guess?"

Brux and the banker lost no time in nodding, but the gleam in the latter's eyes was a bit malevolent, to say the least.

"Then that's all settled," the Smiler sighed. "There's nothin' so admired by God, gents, as lovin' your neighbor. But I've always found that when your neighbor gets too obstreperous there's nothin' like plantin' your fist on his jaw to l'arn him good manners."

Jones blinked. Brux stared open-mouthed.

"An' now let's get to business, gents," Smiling Smith went on, when he felt that his audience was duly impressed with his strange code. "I come out here to Bucksnort to ranch. I bought that old Smithers place for the same laudable purpose. What's more, I'm goin' to run it. An' no straggly-haired, ambition-spurred, money-clutchin' syndicate's gonna stop me! An' you can stick a pin in that!"

Brux, turning to Jones, stretched his long legs uneasily. "Tell 'im."

The banker, thus adjured, spoke hesitantly. "The Big Three, same bein' Brux, Dixon and' Bast, have been usin' the range controlled by the Smithers place a good many years. They don't want to lose that range. They'd have bought from the owner, but couldn't locate him, although you seem to have succeeded in doing so. What will you take for the Smithersplace, Mr. Smith?"

Smith's cold eyes fixed themselves on the banker's pinched features. "I guess you don't hear real well, Mister. I said I'm aimin' to ranch that property, myself. Further, I've put up some barbed wire fences around my range. They're goin' to stay up, too. I got stock on the way here now—bein' shipped in by way of Dog Track."

"Fences! Cripe!" Brux' fishy eyes googled.

"Yuh con't get away with it, Smith!"

"Who says so?"

Si Jones scowled malignantly. "The Big Three's too powerful for you to buck, Mr. Smith," he explained. "They'll smash you flatter than a plate if you get in their way! You are out of luck now, anyway. When Bast an' Dixon come to, they'll be hog-wild to get your scalp. The best thing that you can do is fork your bronc an' fan wind!"

"Not on your tintype!" Smith grinned. A steely glitter, like the glint of sun on a gun-barrel, crept into his cold blue eyes, as he added:

"I'm servin' notice on you jaspers here an' now. Live an' let live, or I'll jam a spoke in your wheel yuh can't yank out!" And, with a final grin, Smiling Smith turned on his heel and stamped from the office without another word.

CHAPTER II

RED HANDED

UPON LEAVING the bank and its private conference which his presence had so rudely interrupted, Smiling Smith turned his boisterous footsteps toward the Tall Bottle Saloon, a resort that was owned on the quiet by Big Al Bast. Passing through the swinging doors, Smith found that not many men were idling away their time therein. Those present, however, were quite sufficient to his needs.

"All up to the bar, gents!" he cried in his heartiest voice. "All up an' drown your sorrows in a cup of good red wine! Drink an' be merry, gents, for tomorow your gullets may be stopped with dust!"

Men looked upon this yellow-haired stranger who talked so queer with a look that his queerness merited, but none hesitated to participate in downing the free drinks he offered.

After paying for a second round of drinks, Smith proceeded to get down to the business that had brought him to the resort. Smiling, he broached his proposition:

"You're gazin', gents, at the new owner of the Smithers place. Yes sir, I've bought it lock, stock, an' barrel! An' I need some hands to help me run it. I aim to make a A-1 spread outa that place. Who's lookin' for a job?"

No one spoke and the silence dragged out painfully. Smith arched his eyebrows as he cocked an enquiring eye over his collection of barroom loafers. "What? Nobody wants a job at top-hand wages?"

Under his searching regard several of the loungers shifted uneasily. One or two gave a last reluctant look at their emptied glasses and turned away. Smith scowled.

"Well, well!" he said tartly. "I never thought to see the day when good jobs at top pay would go a-beggin'."

Finally a heavy-set man spoke up apologetically:

"Yuh see, Mister, it ain't that we don't want to work, nor yet it ain't the fact that we don't wana work for you. But some of us has families to think of, an' them that ain't has a due an' proper regard for the comfort of their necks—"

"Families! Necks!" Smith snorted. "What the heck are you talkin' about?"

"Well, yuh see, Mister, it ain't exackly healthy to buck the syndicate, an' workin' for you on the Smithers place wouldn't be doin' nothin' else but!"

Cold scorn shone from the Smiler's eyes. "Don't tell me you weak-livered gents is scared of a mutton-faced crowd of money-bags like that Big Three outfit! Why, gosh-a'mighty, I just knocked the tar outa that feller Bast an' his sidekick, Dixon! Why, them bluffin' polecats wouldn't even scare a half-growed kid, where I hail from!"

"Mebbe not, Mister, but they make wrecks of full-growed men around here. We don't want no job buckin' that outfit; thanks jest the same. An'," the speaker added in a whisper, "was I you, I wouldn't go round tellin' lies about beatin' up Bast an' Dixon. They won't like it!"

"Did you say *lies?*" Smith took three steps toward the heavy-set speaker who backed precipitately away. With a disgusted grunt, Smith paid for the wine and liquor consumed by the men he'd hoped to hire, and strode disgruntledly from the place.

"Never see such a bunch of ol' women in my life!" he muttered as he headed for the livery stable to get his horse. "Looks like I done picked one gosh-awful country to start my ranch in. Plumb overrun with bullyin' moneybags an' weak-kneed waddies!"

With a snort of disgust, he added: "Maybe I can locate me a couple of rustlers or hawse thieves——I don't reckon such gentry lose much sleep over buckin' the syndicate! Yep, I'll sure have to find me a couple of hard-workin' outlaws to run my spread."

In this frame of mind Smiling Smith was holding discourse with himself when he came in sight of the livery stable where he'd left his horse. Then he came to a sudden stop, fists clenching at his sides.

There before the stable which was situated on a side street, a girl in scarlet rags was struggling in the arms of a tall wiry man with curly black hair. Smith started forward on a run.

As he drew near he saw that the girl's face, a pretty one, was more a picture of rage than fright. She was scratching at the tall man's face with clawing hands that he could not seem to catch.

"Let go, *maldito!* Let loose," she cried, whipping a tiny dagger from her bosom, "or, Mother of God, I weel cut your heart out!"

But before she could raise the blade to a damaging position, the tall man got his arms around her and drew her so tightly to him that Smith could hear the sharp expulsion of breath from her cramped lungs.

"What's goin' on here?" the Smiler demanded, grabbing the stranger by the collar of his shirt and with a surprising demonstration of strength and science shaking him loose of the girl. "What do you think you're doin', anyhow? That's no way to treat a lady!"

"Lady!" the tall man exploded with a short laugh. *"Lady!"*—That's good! She's a damn mestiza wench an' free sport for the man as tames her—an' I'm gonna tame her or break her damn neck"

A faint smile slid across Smith's lips as the man said this; it was a smile that lacked much of being mirthful. He stared the fellow up and down, his blue eyes growing steadily more frosty second by second.

The "tamer of wenches" was a tall man, at the least a good six-foot-two. His hat had been lost in the scuffle and his black hair was curly and well-trimmed. Smith had never liked curly hair on the stronger sex; nor did he like the type of tiny black mustache with which the tall man's handsome darkskinned face was adorned. But these things were as nothing compared to the distaste with which the Smiler observed the tall man's eyes. They were arrogant, ruthless eyes, in the depths of which tiny flecks of fire burned wickedly—killer eyes, they were. And, as though to prove it, the fellow wore a pair of black-butted guns in scarred holsters slung low on his thighs.

"Oh, you're goin' to break her neck, are you?" Smith said, and let his eyes roam to the girl herself. She didn't seem scared, he thought; in fact, she seemed quite calm and collected as she stood at one side watching them with eager gaze while she awaited the outcome of his intervention.

"You heard me," the tall man growled, adding ominously: "An' if you don't trot your meedling self outa this picture quick, I'll break *your* neck as well!"

"That ain't no Christian way to talk," Smith reproved him. "The Good Book says 'Peace on earth, good will among men'—or words tuh that effect. Things like you're sayin' Mister, only leads to bruised knuckles an' sore heads—"

"Clear out, you! Clear out quick! An' don't give me no more of your psalm singin' mouthwash, neither!" growled the tall man, striding forward menacingly. "Hop it!"

"Don't antagonize me that way, Mister," Smith's drawl was hatefully leisured, nicely calculated to enrage the tall man further. His own cold blue eyes gazed straight into the other man's smouldering black ones. For a full five seconds there was silence.

The tall man's eyes abruptly slitted, his head thrust forward vulture-fashion and his hands dropped toward his holstered weapons.

Smiling Smith thought fast. If he let things take their nautral course there could be but one end possible to the present situation—gunplay. He had no gun, himself and so could feel no proper enthusiasm for the other's determination to place him in the role of corpse. Plainly, this was a case where quick and violent action were in demand.

He let his eyes rove round, then suddenly focused them on a point just back of the gun-fighter's wiry, forward-balanced form. The latter, his instinct insisting that he follow the eyes of an enemy in an effort to outguess him, almost turned—almost, but not quite.

"Keep out of this, Bast!" Smith snapped. "I can 'tend to this maverick without no help!" and he scowled as though to discourage interference.

The tall man stabbed a swift glance over his shoulder for a look at the interloper. It was most unfortunate.

With a lightning movement Smith jerked both the fellow's guns from leather, brought them up on flashing arcs and, as the gunman whirled to snatch at emptied holsters, lashed him twice across the head. Two heavy-handed

swipes that drove the guns' front sights beneath their owner's scalp. Without another sound, the tamer of wenches
went down in a crumpled heap.

Smith glared at the people who were witnessing his
prowess from hard won spots of vantage. "If you got any
objections, spit 'em right out," he said.

But evidently no one had. At least, no objections were
voiced.

"The receptions I been gettin' in this country make me
feel real welcome—like a polecat at a church sociable,"
he added pointedly.

The girl in the scarlet rags claimed his attention next.
She was just a chit of a thing, he thought, and young. Her
arms and legs and feet were bare to the sun's bright rays
and tanned to a golden bronze. She wore a gold locket
about her neck on a tiny chain and had big brown eyes that
were soft and soulful. Smith looked closer. Yes, he decided, she was a tempting baggage—small wonder the tall
man had found her attractive.

"Your honor has made the bad enemy," she said, indicating with a negligent foot, the man on the ground.
"Black Potak, the syndicate foreman. He ees the ver' bad
man. He has the oh-so-long memory. Better you get away
from here, *pronto*."

"Shucks, he's harmless enough now," Smith grinned.
"What do they call you, *niña?*"

"Dolo, your honor," she answered, rolling her dusky
eyes.

"Dolo," he repeated with puzzled frown. "Dolo?"

"*Si,* it ees short for Dolores, *señor*." She gave him a
searching glance while with the toes of her left foot she
made little marks in the sand. "Does your honor not like
eet?"

"Oh, I guess it's a good enough name." The Smiler was
only mildly interested in girls, and not at all in their
names. "You better get home before this fella comes to."

"Oh," she laughed, and the sound was wistful, "but I

14

have no home. I am the wanderer—w'at you call 'Gypsy.' But I have the *cuchillo*," she returned the knife to her bosom. "I am no es-cared."

"Humph!" Smith scowled. Her lack of fear would not protect her from Potak. The fellow would be on the rampage and, lacking Smith, would likely vent his rage on her. So Smith thought. Certainly he could not leave her to the tender mercies of Bucksnort's villainous citizens.

"Say!" he exclaimed, struck by a sudden idea. "I got a ranch, the Smithers place. I reckon I could use a sort of housekeeper an' cook. How'd you like the job? 'Course I couldn't pay yuh much," he added hastily, "but I could see that you weren't pestered with guys like this Potak jasper."

"Oh, but it ees too kind of your honor. No, Dolo best stay here. I would only breeng you the trouble, *señor*." But her eyes were bright with interest and, yes, he thought, with longing.

He grinned. "Don't worry about trouble, *niña*. Me an' him's ol' buddies. Er, I don't suppose you got a horse, have yuh? *Caballo?*"

She shook the tawny locks beneath the scarlet bandanna which she wore about her head.

"Well, I'll get you one, *niña de los ojos*," he said, and strode inside the stable, the girl following in his footsteps. There was a curious light in her dusky eyes, but he did not see it, being busy with his thoughts.

But he could not locate the stableman; no doubt the fool had bolted when trouble had seemed imminent. Well, his absence was as useful as his presence. Smith saddled his flea-bitten nag and saddled a dun mare for the girl. Then he crossed to where he saw a battered desk in a far corner. Finding a bit of wrapping paper he scribbled a note to say he was renting the dun mare and left some money with his message on the desk.

Returning to the horses, he found the girl already mounted, her scarlet rags pulled well up toward her slender thighs, exposing considerable creamy skin untouched by the sun's browning rays. Smith looked hastily away.

"Hurry, your honor! Potak—the man is getting up!"

Smith stepped into the saddle and they rode out of the stable's narrow rear door.

As their horses jogged along the trail through the sage that led to the Smithers place, they began to take silent stock of one another. She wasn't really beautiful, he decided, but there was certainly something about her petite brown features that made a gent want to look again. Her skin was a truly wonderful texture and tanned a rich golden brown by the sun. Her tawny hair gleamed coppery in this bright light, and her brown eyes were like deep wells at dusk; wells that invited a man to swim, he thought irrelevantly.

Too, she was not a coward, like those weak-kneed jaspers in the Tall Bottle. She had shown no fear while struggling with the syndicate foreman, only a fierce anger had blazed from her eyes. He found himself deciding that she would have managed to take care of herself pretty well, even if he hadn't come along.

She sat her saddle easily, comfortably. Evidently she had ridden before. She exhibited no false modesty at the necessary exposure of her slender, graceful legs. He found her something of a puzzle, this girl in the scarlet rags.

She watched his seat in the saddle and nodded her head in approval. She searched his face, too, and evidently found that to her satisfaction, for a pleased smile touched her lips when he wasn't looking. And she liked his lazy drawl. But she could not understand why he rode without a gun. It was a phenomenon unusual in the men she had known.

They rode leisurely and talked of this and that.

"Is eet grand, this rancho of your honor's?"

"Oh, so-so," he shrugged. "It ain't so much for looks, but it's stout and the range is somethin' a gent would ride a long ways to get a look at. I expect several of the jaspers in this vicinity to come an' take a look, soon as I get it stocked," he added, sardonically. "It'll be a rare sight around here, I'm thinkin'."

Abruptly there rang out from behind them the thud of pounding hoofs, shouts, oaths, and the faint pop of distant guns. They pulled up and looked around.

"Mira!" the girl cried excitedly. *"Bandidos,* your honor! *Ladrones! Jibaros!"*

"Huh?" Smith said, then drove in his spurs. After all, she might be right, he thought. He did not know this country very well, and what he had so far seen of it and of its citizens did nothing to convince him that she was wrong. "Bandits! Thieves! Killers!" the girl had cried. Well, he could not be surprised if they turned out to be exactly that. It was a heck of a country!

They threw their horses forward at a hard run. The girl's dun mare ran well and with a will, but the Smiler felt misgivings as to the length of its endurance.

Before them lay a tumbled region that looked the final word in desolation. Up-thrust saucer-like basins rose here and yon from the undulating desert floor in reds, yellows, and pale greens. Great chunks of grey-black lava scattered about the sand like a giant's load of coal misplaced.

"We got a chance, gal," Smith told her after twenty minutes of fast riding. But despite the easy smile on his lips, the sharp whiplike timbre of his words informed Dolores that if they had, the chance was mighty slim.

The great expanse of bad lands stretching out to either side and straight ahead for forty miles, was known locally as the Devil's Boot. Almost in its center lay the spot they were making for, an eight-mile valley comprising the lush acreage of the Smithers place—a watered paradise of green amid the desert wastes.

The pace set by Smiling Smith was a swift one for both horses were fresh and the Smiler had had all the trouble he wanted—for one day.

After another ten minutes of hoof-pounding silence,

Smith swung his horse abruptly from the trail, the girl following his lead. Down a sandy slide they slide into the bed of a barranca that cleaved its way past breaks and rippled slides below the level of the desert floor. It was a short cut the Smiler knew, having discovered it that morning by experimenting exploration.

The wind created by the headlong pace of their hard-running mounts pushed against their faces like an invisible hand; stopped their ears to all but the pounding hoofs. Another half hour went jolting by and another break sped up in the barranca wall. Smith reached for the girl's reins as soon as he saw it, and drew both horses to a halt.

"Shh!" he said with a finger across his lips, and for several momonets they remained silent, listening. Smith's bronzed features grew harsh and deep-etched lines showed up about his mouth that made him seem old and tired. The sounds of pursuit were louder, closer than when first heard, and the distant pounding hoofs soon rose to a thunderous rumble that mingled with the whooping yip-yip-yip of the on-coming riders.

"I don't know where that canyon leads," Smith said, indicating the break in the barranca wall, "but I reckon we better try it. The ground's pretty hard here and won't leave much sign. At best them bandits'll have to split up to make sure of us. C'mon, bad as I hate tuh push these nags, we gotta hustle if we're goin' to save our bacon!"

They whirled their lathered mounts and dashed into the side canyon at a fast lope. Its walls grew swiftly higher, its floor let swiftly down. Here and there a few stumpy jack-pines grew, and along the rugged walls an occasional bluish blur marked the sight of a smoke-bush.

The dun mare was blowing now; at her present pace she would not last much longer. Smith slowed their gait —somehow the girl's mount must be kept on its feet and moving. For his flea-bitten nag had never been partial to carrying double loads.

The canyon floor was growing sandy. Scattered clumps of sage appeared, with now and again a smear of puffy, cottony white showing the presence of sharp-thorned cholla, and the red-tipped octopus-like arms of ocatilla.

They paused again to listen; there was no doubt about it—the pursuit was gaining swiftly, and aparently their ruse of turning off had dismally failed. There must, thought Smith, be an expert tracker with the bandits, a man who could read sign from the saddle.

A sharp bend showed in the canyon straight ahead. The Smiler looked at Dolores.

"Ain't much use continuin' this losin' race, gal," he said gruffly. "You go around that bend yonder and keep on goin'. I'm gonna wait right here an' see what this hell-for leather ridin's all about. You—"

"I weel wait with your honor," the girl broke in, her troubled eyes on his. "I am not afraid—weeth you."

Smith flicked her a searching glance. "Good girl," he said. "But if you're aimin' tuh stick with me, I reckon we'll jest meander round yon bend. It might be we'll manage to climb outa this—" he mopped his perspiring face, "darn furnace."

But when they rounded the bend, all thought of escape vanished from their minds. In leaving the main bed of the barranca they had chosen a box-canyon; smooth sandstone walls towered high on either side and before them. The trail was ended, their race was run.

Smith looked at the girl and grinned. "It won't be long now," he said, sardonically.

Presently the roaring pound of their pursuers' hoofs had grown so loud that both the fugitives realized that the bandits' appearance could not much longer be put off.

The rumble of hoofs, like sullen thunder, swept round the bend, and the pursuers in a half-circle drew up before them. They were six.

"So we run yuh down, did we?" the speaker, a large man with a ferocious black mustache trimmed walrus fashion, eyed the Smiler with satisfaction.

Smiling Smith was gazing in open-mouthed astonishment at the star that glinted on the large man's vest. "A
sheriff!" he gasped. "I'll be damned!"

"I guess you will, young fella," the lawman said. "As a
stealer of hawsses an' gals, you'll find this county deals
swift justice. If you got anything to say, hombre, then
you'd better say it quick because in about three minutes
we're gonna start hunting a big tree with a friendly
branch."

Smith loked the posse over swiftly. The stablekeeper
was a member of it, as were several of the Tall Bottle
loafers whom he had treated when trying to hire a crew.
"Just what am I charged with, anyhow?"

The proprietor of the livery stable snickered. Several
others grinned.

"You're charged with kidnappin' that gal an' stealin'
that dun mare she's ridin'," the sheriff said grimly. "An'
it loks like to me, you pretty damn near wore her out—the
mare, I mean."

"Who says I done them things?" Smith's frosty eyes
searched the faces of the posse. He clenched his fists suggestively as he caught the stablekeeper's glance. The man
gulped, looked away uneasily. Then, drawing comfort and
courage from the presence of his brother-posse men, he
growled: "I do—leastways, I claim you stole my mare!"

"What you basin' your argument on?" Smith demanded.
"How the hell can you say I stole your durned nag when
I left a note on your desk sayin' that I was rentin' her an'
leavin' some *dinero* with the note? How you aimin' to get
around that, I'd admire to ask?"

"Note? Money?" The stableman snorted. "I ain't seen
no note, an' I ain't seen no money either—an' what's
more, I don't believe you left 'em. You're jest tryin' to
alibi yourself outa this!"

This was a fine fix, Smith reflected grimly. Then an idea
struck him:

"What made you think it was me that took your nag if you didn't get my note?"

"Potak, the syndicate foreman, saw you take the mare an' saw you force the girl to mount 'er," the stableman retorted hotly. "An' what's more, when he tried to stop you, you lashed him across the head with your gun-barrell! Don't try lyin' out of it, because the sheriff an' me both saw his wounds. Why, it's a wonder you didn't kill him!"

The sheriff nodded grim agreement.

Smith laughed shortly. "So that's the way of it, eh?" Potak had certainly played him a scurvy trick, he thought, for there was no doubt in his mind that the syndicate foreman had not only twisted the truth to suit his crafty self, but had very likely appropriated Smith's note and money as well.

He wasted no time in berating Potak, however. What the foreman had done was merely to pay him back with interest for the pistol whipping Smith had given him. And the code of paying back all injuries with interest whenever possible was the self-same code by which Smith lived himself. An eye for an eye was the Smiler's motto, and if he got himself out of this jam he meant to see that more grief came Potak's way.

"Well, if that's all you got to say," the sheriff broke in upon his thought, "I make a motion we go look for a big tree. The sooner we string you up, young fella, the sooner I can get back to town. An' I'm gettin' hungry fast."

"I got more to say, all right, an' I aim to say it *pronto*." The Smiler's glance grew stern and frosty as he eyed the stableman. "Did Potak say I hit him over the head with my gun-barrel?"

"He sure did!"

"Then he's a mangy, straggly-haired, polecat liar!" Smith snapped. "I ain't wearin' no gun an' I ain't thrown no gun away because I haven't been wearin' any to throw away. An' you can prove it by him an' him an' him!" he pointed out three of the posseman he had treated in the Tall Bottle. "They saw me this mornin' an' they know I didn't have no gun. An' if their word an' mine ain't good enough for the law o' this blasted county, you can prove I didn't have no gun by Si Jones, Al Bast, Jud Dixon an' that tight-mouthed fella Brux."

"But," the sheriff protested, "I saw them wounds on Potak's head an' they sure were made by the sight on a gun-barrel. He was pistol-whipped an' you can't tell me different. If you ain't the hombre that did it, I'd like to know who did!"

"That's for you an' him to figger out," Smith grinned, feeling that he now held the upper hand.

But the sheriff was not yet ready to admit himself defeated. "All this talk," he growled, "ain't changin' the evidence of that mare an' the gal bein' in your possession. We've caught you red-handed, young fella, an'—"

"What about the note I left with the money on the desk in this fella's stable?"

"We didn't find any note and we didn't come across no money. And I only got your word that you left some. Any gent in your position would say the same. I reckon you're guilty, all right."

"But," the girl spoke up for the first time, "he did! Weeth my own eyes I saw heem write the note an' place the *dinero* weeth it on the desk like he say. He have keednapped me sure enough, but I could not see heem accuse' of somet'ing he deed not do!"

Sheriff Dan Hellman gave Dolores a sharp look. At last he said: "All right, sister, we'll take your word for it. If he wants to *buy* the horse now, to show his good faith, we'll let him out of the horse-stealin' charge—"

"What? Me buy that busted-down nag?" Smith growled. "I sh'd say not!"

"Well, look at 'er!" the stableman wailed. "You've plumb ruined her, runnin' her like you did on a day like this—jest look at 'er heave!"

"You're addressin' them remarks of yours to the wrong party," Smith flicked a thumb toward the sheriff, who was fingering his ferocious lip-adornment. "That's the gent you want to talk to, fella. If him an' the rest of yuh hadn't taken after us like a bunch of Commanche Injuns on the warpath, your dun mare wouldn't of had no reason to be heavin' the way she is. Talk to the sheriff, brother. The county'll pay for your nag. If I wasn't so dang soft-hearted, I'd soak the county somethin' for the wear an' tear on my own cayuse!"

"You better sing low, young fella," the sheriff hissed ominously. "I ain't done with you, yet. Just 'cause this gal swears yuh outa horse-stealin' ain't savin' youre bacon on the kidnappin' charge. Tie him up, boys, an' we'll hunt for that tree."

Smith's airy spirits took a drop. What had ever possessed the girl to say that he had kidnapped her? The ungrateful baggage! He should have let Potak have her!

Then abruptly his mind did a somersault; he saw now why she'd said that. Her testimony anent the money and note for the rest of the mare would have been disregarded had she seemed an interested party. But what did it avail him to be cleared of horse stealing, if they were going to hang him for kidnapping: his neck was to get a stretching either way. He was in a tough spot and no mistake!

As the sheriff's men began to tie his hands, Dolores of the scarlet rags came once again to his assistance:

"Meester Sheriff!" so plaintively she said it, that the big Dan Hellman turned. He arched his brows and waited. "Please, Meester Sheriff, don' hang my man. *Señor* Smeeth is the one fine hombre. He hos tol' me he will take me to his *rancho grande* an' make marry weeth me—

"What?" the sheriff looked astounded. "You mean to tell me Smith has asked you to *marry* him. *You!*"

Dolores' grave brown eyes roved slowly over her person, rag by scarlet rag; only now, it seemed, was she realizing that the stranger's proposal might be some ghastly jest! Smith, whose wide mouth had come mighty near sagging open in amazement at the girl's startling revelation, suddenly turned away his head as Dolores' big brown eyes grew misty and a tear rolled down his cheek.

Even he, knowing better, had almost been convinced by this self-styled Gypsy's clever acting. What wonder then if Sheriff Dan Hellman swallowed her tale hook, line and sinker?

The lawman, of course, could not know that Dolores was but acting. He sat there gaping in red-faced consternation at the havoc his brutal words appeared to have wrought.

"Uh—er—Gosh, don't cry, Miss!" he stammered helplessly. "I—I spoke a bit hasty-like, I reckon, ma'am. I—I sure am sorry. Gosh! See!" he exclaimed with not wholly-simulated joy when Smith, leaning from his saddle, placed a consoling arm around Dolores' slender form, drew her tearwet cheek to his shoulder. "I was wrong about it—plumb wrong. Of course Smith loves yuh, Miss, I—I reckon I've made a mistake all round."

He blew his nose vigorously as his men turned their mounts toward the homeward trail. Then he bowed with a gallant flourish of his dusty sombrero to the girl and Smiling Smith and, urging the reluctant stableman before him, departed—leaving the love-birds in quiet and peace, absolved of every charge.

CHAPTER III

A POTENT LORD

THE NEXT few days passed slowly in the ordinary chores of a stockless ranch. But Smith was busy most of the time and around the house but seldom. Dolo had proved to be a diligent house keeper and the Smiler liked her first rate.

But he'd like her a whole lot better, he told himself, if she didn't look at him so funny every once in a while. Like as if he'd forgotten to feed her, or something. It wasn't right.

And then one morning she announced that the house needed cleaning, and just because he chose to sleep in the bunkhouse every night was no good reason why he shouldn't help her. When he hinted that he'd ought to inspect the fences on the south range. she said "Damn!" And so, because he wished to make a lady of her and felt that ladies shouldn't swear, Smith gave in at last and consented to do his share.

"Breeng the car-pets in the *casa*."

"*Si, niña de los ojos*," Smith grinned and picking up the carpets carried them inside.

"Why do you call me 'darling of the lovely eyes' when you do not loff me?" Her voice was plaintive, her glance was grave. "Ever since we came here have I waited for you so say 'Soon now we get married, *niña*, an' all you say was 'Pretty sleek treeck you play on the sheriff!' Sometimes I'm theenk I tear your hair out, so mad I get."

Smith dropped the carpets and eyed her in amazement. "Huh? Well, for the love of Mike, I never said I loved yuh, did I? Well, what are yuh kickin about, then? Didn't I save you from that Potak polecat?"

"An' deed I not save you from the sheriff?" her brown eyes flung reproach at him. "An' deed I not do eet by tell' heem you weesh to marry weeth me? Deed I not? What you theenk he say when he fin' out you haff not done eet, eh?"

"But, sufferin' sidewinders, gal! I ain't in love with anybody—an' I don't want to be! I ain't the marryin' kind!" And, snorting at the very notion that he might be, Smith strode outside leaving Dolores to finish the housecleaning by herself.

He was in a mood to feel the noon-day heat, and he felt it.

"Gosh," he muttered, "all women ever think about, seems like, is love! It's enough to drive a fella frantic! Maybe the climate has somethin' tuh do with it. I betcha it ain't no hotter on the Mojave Desert than it is right here in my own dooryard. I bet the people what's been brought up in this climate has to feed their chickens cracked ice tuh keep 'em from layin' hard-boiled eggs!"

Presently, however, the Smiler's thoughts turned from women and the climate. He was sitting in the doorway, feet scuffing at the sand on the ground outside. He wondered why old Smithers, original builder of this great adobe house, had ever made it so strong and thick. "Musta been expectin' to hole up here if the Law got to doggin' his trail too close," he decided finally.

"Why, gosh, just look at the work he must have put into this door—solid oak an' a full six inches thick!" It was. Besides that, it was a bit wider than the usual custom in that region, and stood a good eight feet high.

"What a door! An' bound with strips of hammered iron! He sure took pains to get himself the best, all right. I bet Smithers was a gay ol' dawg—what a life he musta led!"

Beyond doubt Smithers *had* led a rather adventurous existence, if Dame Rumor came anywhere near the truth. Smithers, it was said, had been a stagecoach robber in his palmy days; chief of as villainous a crew as ever slit a purse or wrecked a stage. He had operated in the vicinity of Bucksnort for nearly five years before the Law finally had ended his notorious career with the aid of a hempen necktie. But whether Smithers had actually robbed travelers of the highway or whether he had been the scapegoat for someone else, must ultimately have mattered little to the man himself. For certainly he had been hung. There were loafers in Bucksnort who, for a quarter, would gladly point out to visitors the very tree on which the posse had wound up Smithers' career.

The wandering thoughts of Smiling Smith were abruptly disturbed. The soft *clup-clup* of an approaching rider drew

Smith's eyes to the dusty trail. A slight frown crossed his saturnine features.

"Ha! A potent lord comes yonder—as the book says."

The only thing apparently potent about the approaching horseman was the six-gun reposing in the worn holster tied to his leg, and the potency of that was a thing yet to be learned. He was clad in a patched red-and-black checked flannel shirt and a pair of frazzled corduroy trousers tucked into scuffed range boots. A blue neckerchief was pulled tight about the scrawny neck, a floppy-brimmed sombrero was shoved far back on his shaggy head.

"Howdy, pilgrim. Light down an' rest your nag," Smith invited hospitably.

The stranger grinned. "Thirsty weather, ain't it?"

"A bit warmish," Smith admitted. "Travelin' far?"

"No farther than I hev to. It depends—" he mopped his forehead with a grimy hand. "I'm a gent as growed up in the saddle, Mister. I'm lookin' for a job—"

"Job! Good gosh, what for? I didn't know that gents ever worked in this country! Ain't you afraid the syndicate won't like it?"

"Hmmm. Wal, hunger drives a cruel spur," the stranger said apologetically. "Tranter's the name, Mister—Buck Tranter, at yer service."

"Glad tuh know you," Smith stretched forth a hand. "I'm Smith."

"Smith? . . . . Not the jigger what broke up the Wheatley gang? Not Smilin' Smith, by ary chance?"

"Yeah—but don't tell anyone. I'm tryin' to live peaceful."

"Wal, prancin' prairie chickens! Where's yore guns?"

"Guns?" Smith scowled. "What do I want with guns? Gosh! Live in peace an' love your neighbors—even syndicates. That's my motto."

"Yeah, an' yer tombstone's apt tuh read: 'He loved his neighbors—but it was no insurance ag'in' a hunk o' lead.'" Arms akimbo, the ragged stranger stared at Smith reprovingly. "Why, this country's plumb lousy with outlaws —outlaws an' politicians what sure oughta be. An, here's you tryin' to hog this spread without no guns! Hell! I hope you got your coffin ordered!"

"Shucks," replied the gaunt Smiler, quite unruffled.

Unhooking one grimy hand from his belt, Tranter produced a plug of tobacco and bit off a generous chew. "Lissen, Smilin' Smith, to a man what knows. Step soft an' careful around here, or all them friends of yourn back in Painted Stick will have a sure-enough chance tuh walk behind yuh slow an' mournful-like—tuh Boot Hill!"

But Smith only grinned his own grin. "Lookin' for a job, eh? Will yuh work?"

"Work!" Tranter snorted and looked insulted. "Say! I'm knowed far an' wide as a fella what welcomes work with open arms. Yeah, an' what I mean a big smile!"

"Well, all I gotta say is, your clothes shore don't look like you ever made much money at it," Smith said skeptically.

"Nope, they don't," Tranter shook his head dolefully. "The rewards of work an' virtue aroun' this neck of the wods is sure some meagre. But I can work, all right. Yes, sir! I'm a early riser what don't bed down till way past midnight account of I'm allus so busy doin' the work other cowhands ducks!"

"Humph!" Smith said. "It sounds too good to be anywheres near the truth. But I'll tell you, Tranter; I'm sort of aimin' to get me one or two upright scoundrels what I can trust—"

"Yuh won't have to hunt long for such gentry in this country, I can tell yuh. I've turned one or two deals in the course o' my experience what netted me pretty fair returns, Smith. But I'll have tur admit there's so many dang crooks around Bucksnort I've come right-down near tuh starvin' to death. The competition's wicked!"

Smith grinned. "Yeah, they do run pretty ornery, hereabouts. What I want, though, is a couple of hellions I can *trust.* The Big 3 has used this spread for a free feed long enough. I've fenced it an' warned 'em off."

"I can see a gun squabble loomin' large on the horizon." There was a faraway look in Tranter's eyes. "Smoke, hellfire an' brimstone," he grinned.

"Gosh, I sure hope not," Smith said hastily. "A feller ought to live in peace an' raise children like the Good Book says—" he broke off abruptly, shot a fearful look inside the house, then grinned with relief. Dolores was not in sight.

"Er, can you use that smoke-pole you're totin'?" he asked Tranter.

The ragged stranger grinned. *"Can* I? I ain't one for braggin', Smiler, but as a fast-shootin' ranny, I'm the genu-wine article; a holster-hopper on which you kin smell the powder-smoke!"

The gaunt man chuckled. "You're a sight too modest, Tranter. Where's your crown?"

"Crown?"

"The king of braggers ought to have a crown just like any other king," said Smith, and laughed. "Gettin' down to brass tacks though, an' talkin' turkey, have yuh ever worked with sheep?"

"Huh?" the ragged stranger stiffened. "Did I hear right?" Turning slowly in all directions he cautiously sniffed the air. Then he relaxed. "Gosh, you durned near stampeded me that time, Smiler. *Sheep!* I hate the very sight o' the blattin' critters!"

Smith fetched a doleful sigh. "Well, this here's a sheep farm you're standin' on. At any rate, it will be as soon as my three carloads of woolies gets here."

Tranter shoved back his hat, the better to scratch his shaggy mane. Standing thus, he gave the Smiler a long-careful scrutiny. Then he shook his head. "I can't under-stand it; you shore don't *look* like no blattin' sheepman."

"Well, I sh'd hope not!" Smith snapped indignantly. "I'm a cowman, fella. But sheep I'll have, if I have to tend

29

'em myself. It's the first step, Tranter, in my fight against the powers-that-be."

"Ye-ah? Wal—"

"An' to a not-too-particular gent, which savvies what end of a gun the smoke curls outa, I'm figgerin' to pay about one hundred a month an' found."

Tranter's eyes popped open. "Wal, strike me pink if I ain't the jasper! Cripes! I'd herd polecats fer them there wages! I—" he came to a sudden pause, peered intently toward a distant hogback, then slowly shook his head. "I *thought* I saw a hat meanderin' along that ridge," he explained, "but I reckon I was mistook. Musta been one of them optical diffusions what yuh read about."

"Yeah, I reckon. Here, sit down on the doorstep with me an' give your feet a rest," Smith invited, moving over. Tranter did so, and for a while they sat in silence.

"You gone to sleep, Smiler?" Tranter asked at last.

"Huh? . . . . No, I been thinkin'. I wonder is there any reason or law to stop me from runnin' this spread as a dude ranch on the side?"

"Dude ranch! Jumpin' gophers! what do yuh wanta do that for?"

"Well, I need the money, for one thing, an' I've heard dude ranches are wonderful profit-hatchers. No expense, no outlay to speak of, except for advertisin', an' everything yuh charge them poor dudes for is clear profit. They say it beats cattle ranchin' all to a frazzle, Tranter."

"Mebbe it does," the ragged gun-toter admitted reluctantly, "but I'd shore hate to play wet-nurse to a bunch of dang dudes. I heard of a dude oncet, what thought bulldoggin' was the name of a Spanish dance!"

Smith chuckled. "That's nuthin'. One time when I was stayin' at the Orient Hotel in Pecos, I was talkin' with a friend an' happened tuh mention that my chaps was gettin' right-down awful. Up steps a dude drummer an' says: 'Friend, what you need is a bottle of skin lotion.'"

Tranter looked at him sideways, shot an amber stream

of tobacco juice at a passing tumblebug, and remarked in an aggrieved voice: "I didn't know this conversation was supposed to be a liar's contest."

Smith grinned. "Well, what do you think of my idea."

"I don't like it. Dudes may be cheap to wrangle, but they shore do get a powerful lot o' work out of a fella. Take my advice an' leave 'em be."

"But I gotta make some quick money, somehow. I spent about everything I had buyin' this property from that Crane Jasper what bought it from the State. Besides, them sheep I got comin' ain't completely paid for yet, an' I'll have a note comin' due on 'em in a coupla months. Then, too, I gotta pay you an' my housekeeper your wages."

"D'yuh mean to say you got a housekeeper on this spread?"

"Yep. A gal named Dolores—an' don't let me catch yuh makin' eyes at her, neither!"

"Huh! yuh needn's worry about *me* makin' eyes at her! I got three wives now, an' three's a-plenty—all I hope is, they don't none of 'em locate me!"

Smith stuck out his hand. "Brother, you sure been around."

"Yeah," said Tranter, shaking it vigorously. "I've seen a thing or two."

"Let's see, now," Smith fetched a bit of wrapping paper and the stub of a pencil from his pocket. "How d'you reckon I oughta word this ad?"

"So you're plumb set on that dude business, are yuh?"

"I reckon. I can't think of no other way to make money fast—"

"What're you figgerin' to charge them critters?"

"Oh, I sh'd say about fifty bucks a day would be a fair price—everything furnished."

"What do yuh mean, everything furnished?"

"Well, grub three a day; a hawss to ride; a bunk to sleep or rest in, an' permission to fish in any o' the lakes hereabouts."

"Humph! I didn't know there was any."

"I don't think there is—but the tourist ads always mentions 'em."

"Cripes! An' you're figgerin' to charge them misguided dudes fifty dollars just to ride on one of them bone-rack nags I seen out in the corral, an' tuh sleep on one o' them pine-slat shelves built ag'in the bunkhouse wall, an' your permission to fish in a lake what ain't got no existence? Well, all I got to say is, any dang dude what's fool enough to spend fifty bucks fer that, deserves jest what he gets!"

"Shucks," Smith chided, "the more yuh charge dudes, an' the less yuh give them, the better they likes yuh."

"They shore must enjoy gettin' close to nature," Tranter muttered. "What're yuh goin' to do if your dudes don't like sheep—or the perfume therefrom?"

"Oh, they won't kick about such trifles. What they want is to see how a real ranch is run, out here in the wild an' woolly West. If I didn't have no sheep to show 'em, they'd feel like they was gettin' gypped."

"Huh! What are yuh goin' to do if they wanta see some honest-to-Gawd cattle?"

"I'll take 'em out an' show 'em some syndicate cattle. Cattle, Tranter, is cattle. They won't never know the difference."

"Wal, I hope not. I'd hate tuh see yuh get sued for missrepresentation."

"Never heard of her," said Smith, with a grin. After a moment he looked up from his scribbling. "How does this sound? 'S Bar S Ranch, Bucksnort, New Mexico. A typical old-time ranch that is actually in operation. 3 carloads of sheep, an' many on nearby ranges. Riding horses for use of guests. Accommodations for four persons; hot an' cold water; warm climate; permission to fish an' hunt. Rates eighty dollars a week or three hundred per month.' "

Tranter shook his head admiringly. "Marv'lous," he said solemnly.

"Well, I believe in bein' truthful," Smith said.

"So I notice. That part about the huntin' an, fishin' is right cute, Smiler. But how yuh goin' to explain that 'hot an' cold water'?"

"Well, most all the water's hot, for a fact," Smith admitted. "But we can put some up in desert bags what'll be cold enough for anyone's fancy. I didn't say it was runnin' water."

"Well, it sounds all right. I hope it'll work.

"Of course it'll work; I only hope too many dudes don't answer this ad. It'd hurt me mighty much to have to turn any of 'em down. Now, here's your first job, Buck. Take this ad to Bucksnort an' telegraph it to one of the El Paso papers. Here's some money—an' don't spend it all on likker."

CHAPTER IV

THE MAN FROM EL PASO

Two weeks slid by with the effortless ease that weeks have upon the desert. Nothing in this length of time happened to disturb the bucolic existence of life on the S Bar S. Apparently the Big Three were content to bide their time. Leastways, such was the Smiler's assumption.

In one another, Smith and his hired man found kindred souls—two hearts that, upon occasions, beat as one. Both agreed that the syndicate needed a lesson. Range hogs were out of fashion, and the Big Three should be made aware of the fact. One thing, however, disturbed the Smiler's equanimity. He was not progressing in his efforts to make a lady out of Dolo. She obstinately refused to conform to any pattern or standard set up for her by Smith. All her spare time was taken up in attempts to manoeuvre the Smiler into matrimony—so far with little more results to show than had his attempts to make of her a lady.

To this extent was she successful: Smith never failed to be conscious of her proximity. Nor had he failed to note that, when she wished to, she could use remarkably good English, all things considered. It was only when she was angry or excited that she relapsed into her deplorable patois. And she had found an excellent way to make him uncomfortable. As he told Tranter.

"When she gives me that reproachful, dyin' calf expression, I feel like goin' out an' shootin' myself!"

But all and all, the three got along together nicely.

Then came a day when once again Smith had an itch for town.

Confiding in Tranter that he was going to see if he could get a loan from Banker Jones, after an early lunch the Smiler set out.

But, though he would not think of admitting it even to himself, Smith's main reason for this abrupt hankering for town was an endeavor to get away from his entrancing housekeeper for a spell. He was beginning to believe she had a bad effect on him. *Something* certainly was keeping his nerves on the raw, and in all justice he could not truthfully lay it at the Big Three's door. Too, his once hearty appetite was falling off alarmingly. And he was becoming prey to fits of melancholy; gloomy, morbid spells in which he felt like laying his neck on a railroad track.

He must be thinking of Dolores too much, he concluded as he rode toward town.

He could not understand why her presence should prove so disturbing a factor to his existence. Other women he had known had not affected him this way!

It was downright humiliating! Be his thoughts never so serious, to his growing consternation he would find them abruptly scattering before the radiant golden face of his ragged, illiterate housekeeper!

"Gosh!" he muttered testily. "What's she want t'have such a hauntin' face for? Why does she have such fetchin' ways? Such a—a—a come-hither smile? Dammit, I ain't the marryin' kind! I couldn't stand bein' tied down to a woman's apron-strings. Lord no! Smilin' Smith wears no gal's frills an' flounces!"

He glowered about him savagely. "I won't be at the beck an' call of no durn woman!"

And in his innocence, the Smiler really believed it.

It was in this frame of mind that the vaunted spittin', cussin' two-fisted he-man entered the sleepy-looking town of Bucksnort that sunny afternoon.

Tethering his flea-bitten nag to the hitching rail fronting the Cowman's Bank, the Smiler stopped to send a malignant glance toward the side-street leading to Ed Kallis' livery stable. It would get no more of *his* business, he told himself grimly.

Entering the bank he came face to face with a man who was leaving—Big Al Bast.

"Huh! You still in the country?"

The Smiler's grin was mocking. "Why not? I ain't seen nobody yet what's big enough to chase me out."

"You'll be singin' different before I get through with yuh."

"Listen, Mister; don't get me wrong," said Smith with sober face. "I'm as Gawd-fearin' a peace-lovin' gent as you'll find in a ten days' ride. I'm plumb overflowin' with the milk of human kindness—*et al.,* as they say in the books. But don't crowd my good nature. I can usually manage to turn the other cheek—up to a certain point. After that I start in bustin' things."

Bast was a heavy-set, burly-looking man with massive shoulders, great long hairy arms and a pair of heavy-muscled barrel-stave legs. Having very little shoulders like a toad on a lumpy rock. His black-stubbled face was fat with padded cheeks and a thick-lipped mouth. At Smith's remarkable speech, he snorted derisively.

"You're a tough egg, all right," he admitted. "But I guess you'll soon learn you ain't quite tough enough to buck the Big Three." He paused a moment as though studying Smith's sober features, then added softly: "Besides, we got the law on our side, fella."

"You can have it," Smith said magnanimously. "My fists is law enough for me. An' when they ain't, I got somethin' home what'll settle all arguments—permanent. Think it over real well, Bast, before you go startin' somethin' you can't finish." And with that parting shot, Smiling Smith strode past the thick-set syndicate man and moved toward the private office of Banker Si Jones.

When Smith entered the bank president's private office, Si Jones looked up nervously from his paper-littered desk and eyed his visitor in some surprise. His pinched features seemed to pale a trifle, and his gimlet mouth closed tighter than the tightest shell of the proverbial clam.

The Smiler, uninvited, drew up a chair and sat down. "How's business, Jones?"

The banker's sleepy lids winked up and he shot a searching glance at his visitor's face. Then his sharp little eyes ducked back behind their screens of flesh.

"Business is all right," he said grudgingly.

"Glad to hear it," boomed Smith heartily, " 'Cause I'd like to make a loan."

"Huh! A—a loan, did you say?"

"That's right, Jones; your hearin's great. I want to make a loan of about—"

"It don't make no difference to me how much you want to borrow, Mister Smith," Si Jones cut in. "The bank is not making any loans on the Smithers place."

Smith, hands on hips, a speculative light in cold blue eyes, asked:

"Why? Don't tell me yuh don't make loans—after all, a bank ain't nothin' but a glorified pawn shop, Mister Jones. Why can't you loan money on the Smithers place? It's got some of the best range in this part of the state—"

"I know what it's got an' what it hasn't got a good deal better than you do," the banker snapped, "and I'm not making any loans on it today."

"Well, how about tomorrow?"

"Nor tomorrow. Nor the next day; nor any other day as long as you're in control there. In other words, I won't lend *you* a red cent no matter what you offer to put up!"

"Oh, so that's the way the wind blows?" Smith grinned sardonically. "You an' the Big Three have decided to freeze me out, have yuh? Well, there's other banks in the state——"

"But I don't think they'll be lending money on the Smithers place just now," Si Jones said smugly. "It's a pretty risky proposition with things in such a unsettled condition hereabouts."

Smith nodded slowly. "Yeah, I can see where you're right about things bein' in an unsettled condition. They're gonna get worse, too, before they get better. Most *any* property around Bucksnort would be a pretty poor investment just now, I reckon. Well, if you ain't in a money-lendin' frame of mind, I guess I'll amble along."

"Say, I wanted to ask you something, Smith. Did you ever hear of any S Bar S ranch?"

"S Bar S?" Smith screwed his features into a knot of perplexity. "S Bar S. . . . now where have I heard that combination before. Ah, what makes yuh ask?"

"Well, there's been a funny-lookin' jasper hanging round town all morning looking for a conveyance to the S Bar S —wherever that is. By the way he talks, I reckon it's a dude ranch of some sort. Say, there's the fella now!" Peering out through the street window, Jones jerked a skinny finger toward a man in a neatly-pressed suit of blue serge store clothes who was crossing the street. The man wore a derby hat, which was attracting due attention.

"Yep, that's the pilgrim," Jones said, grinning. "Ain't he a sight for sore eyes? He come in here this mornin' an' says 'Listen buddy; can you tell——' "

But Smiling Smith had heard enough. Grabbing up his hat, he jerked open the office door and went dashing through the bank as though his chances of heaven lay in getting out of the institution just as fast as Shank's mare would carry him.

Once outside the bank, Smith sprinted across the dusty street and onto the board walk that flanked its other side. "Hey!" he yelled, and the stranger came to a halt.

The Smiler dashed up, grinning broadly. He grabbed the fellow's hand and, shaking it vigorously, worked it up and down like a pump handle, much to the other man's surprise.

"Say, what the heck?" ejaculated he of the derby hat. "Just what's—"

"My name's Smith, an' I'm right proud tuh meet up with you, Mister—"

"Monahan's my name," said the stranger, with a hard stare. "What kind of a confidence game are you up to buddy?"

"Huh?" Smith gave the fellow an appraising stare. The stranger's feet were encased in a pair of yellow shoes, rather dusty at the moment, but undoubtedly new. His blue serge suit was not so new and, though neatly pressed, was a bit shiny in places. His black derby, cocked at a jaunty angle, topped a face that was red, freckled, and considerably more sophisticated than were the general run of visages to be encountered in the New Mexican town of Bucksnort. And he had green eyes, that just now were hard and mocking, plus a broken nose.

"I said what kind of a bunco game are you figuring to to work me for?" the stranger paraphrased. "I may be a dude, but I ain't exactly dumb."

Smith grinned. "Sorry, pilgrim. I guess it did kinda look like I was aimin' to play you for a sucker. But I wasn't. I'm Smith—owner of the S-Bar-S."

"Oh," the stranger chuckled. "Well, I'm glad you're here at last. This is the dumbest place I ever struck. What's the matter with these hicks? Every time I asked how to get to the S-Bar-S, these rubes looked at me like I was looney!"

"They sorta got a mad on at me," Smith said, and let it go at that. He saw no reason to enlighten the dude to the fact that his ranch was known to citizens of Bucksnort as the "Smithers place." What this Monahan didn't know certainly couldn't hurt him.

"Reckon I'll have to hunt you up a horse—the road 'tween here an' the ranch ain't what you might call real partial to wagons," Smith said. "You can ride, can't you?"

"Say, when I belonged to the National Guard, I was the best rider in El Paso," Monahan told him frankly.

"Hmm. Well, I'm glad to hear it," the Smiler was relieved. "These broncs at the livery stable are a little frisky; but they're all right if you use a firm hand an' let 'em know you're the boss."

He led the way toward the stable. Not that he wanted to do any further business with Kallis, its proprietor, but because there was no other place in town where he could rent a horse.

Kallis gave him a fishy stare when he and Monahan entered the stable. Smith wasted no time on introductions but came at once to the point. "I want to rent a nag for his gent," he said, peeling out a roll of bills. "An' if you're in a selling frame of mind, I'll buy that dun mare off'n you, seein' as I don't want no hard feelings over her."

"That dun mare will cost you fifty dollars," said Kallis promptly.

"That dun mare," corrected Smith, "ain't worth no more than ten dollars to a glue factory, an' a blacksmith wouldn't give more than five to use her for a bellows."

"Well, it's your fault, dang yuh! If Dan Hellman wasn't the spineless critter he is—"

"Let's not bring that up," Smith cut in hastily. "I'll give you twenty-five bucks for her, cash, an' we'll call that episode finished. How's that?"

"It's a deal," Kallis mopped his brow. "Let's see the color of your money."

Smith paid him, got a bill of sale, ambled around the

stable eyeing the "renters" in the stalls. Presently he spied
a strawberry roan that had not been there when he'd
picked the dun mare for Dolores. The roan's long legs and
deep chest promised plenty of speed, though possibly an
uncomfortable ride for a greenhorn. But heck, Smith
thought, the dude had said he could ride, so what the hell?"

"I'll take this one," he told Kallis, and paid him in a
couple days. Get a saddle on 'im."

While the stableman was doing so, Smith stood in the
doorway looking down the street. Presently he saw what
he had been afraid of seeing: two men walking rapidly
toward the stable. And even at that distance—they were
still a good two blocks away—Smith could see the dark
scowls that ruffled the oncomer's faces. The men were
Potak and Bast, and their stride showed determined purpose.

"All ready," Kallis called.

"Swell!" Smith turned to Monahan. "You ain't got a
gun, have yuh?"

"Gun? Yeah, sure I got one—why?" he eyed the Smiler
curiously.

"No reason special. I was just wonderin'. Can yuh
use it?"

"I used to be a dick in El Paso," Monahan grinned, and
his broken nose wriggled like a rabbit's. "I've got my men."

"Uh-huh. Well, we better be gettin' started," Smith said,
and added confidentially: "There's a couple of jaspers
headed this way I ain't real anxious to palaver with. I
think mebbe we better leave by the rear door there."

To Monahan he presently shouted above the thunderous
sound of beating hoofs: "I'm a buckaroo what knows when
the better part of valor is to run like the devil on horse-
back! Them gents behind is a heap too anxious to catch
up. They wanta talk with me an' they are the kind which
loves to palaver with hot lead an' gunsmoke. But *me,* I'm
different. I'm a gent what believes in lovin' his neighbors—
even when yuh have to bat 'em over the head to do it!"

CHAPTER V

BAD FOR WEAK HEARTS

THE glowing sun sank red and swiftly toward the distant horizon, gilding the far sandstone spires, the bad lands' upthrust empty basins and desolate mesas with lavish prodigality. The broken country put on its evening wraps of saffron, indigo, lavender, orange, cobalt and violet.

In the old abode ranch house at the Smithers place, Dolores gaily cleared the supper things away. The man from El Paso lounged lazily beside the fireplace in the sitting rom, staring into the dancing flames sent up by the grease-wood branches crackling merrily therein and wafting a pleasant fragrance throughout the house.

It was getting cool outside, yet there sat Tranter and the Smiler in back-tilted chairs on the veranda. There was a battered pungent pipe between Buck Tranter's lips and restlessness in his glance. And there was a fay-away look in the squinted eyes with which the Smiler studied the distant desert.

The sun had nearly dropped from sight and the badlands had exchanged their vivid wraps for colors of more somber hue, when against the darkening scarlet sky a buzzard went circling slowly on silent wings.

Interest came to Tranter's glance. "Somethin' dead out there."

Smith puffed his pipe in silence, nodded and puffed again.

Tranter regarded him reproachfully. "You're the most awf'lest dang slavedriver ever I worked for, Smith," he muttered meaningly. "I'm gettin' so fed up with your durned overbearin', money-grubbin' ways I feel a heap like quittin' this spread right now."

Smith grinned. "Well, don't quit yet, ol' son. Things are

gonna happen around here sudden—don't ever doubt it."

"Huh! I been here two weeks already an' ain't done nothin' more strenuous in all that time than take a ad to Bucksnort an' see that it was telegraphed to El Paso. A heck of a life, I calls this; I'm like tuh die of dry rot or petrification, or somethin'! Yellow-Shoes the answer to yer ad?"

"Yeah," Smith answered absently. "An' ex-dick from El Paso, an' a hard-ridin' cargo." Abruptly his soft drawl took on significance. "Company headin' this way."

"Where?" Tranter showed sudden interest.

"Down there," Smith pointed a long lean finger toward the valley's entrance from the desert. "Three hombres. Take 'em about an hour to get here, I reckon."

Tranter leaned back again. "What I'd like to know," he said, "is when them dang woolies of yourn is due to get here."

"They ought to arrive in Bucksnort via the A. T. & S. F. in about three days. We're goin' to have our work cut out gettin' them sheep over the trail. I'm goin' to hunt me up a sheepherder to drive 'em in. You an' me wouldn't be much use at it."

For some time then they sat in silence, each busy with his thoughts. Presently, the night having grown uncomfortably cool, they got up and went inside where Dolores had lighted the lamps in the sitting rom. They could hear Monahan talking to her in the kitchen and the occasional lilt of her soft gay laughter. Smith scowled.

"Did yuh warn that dude about makin' eyes at your filly?" Tranter grinned.

"Go to blazes!" said Smith inelegantly, and dropped into a cowhide chair by the fire.

"Guess you'll be sleepin' in the house now, won't yuh?"

"No," Smith said curtly. "The dude will bunk with us in the bunkhouse."

"Does he know it yet? Eighty bucks a week is a big price for poundin' yer ear on a pine-slat bunk."

Smith stood up, began rolling up his sleeves.

"Here, here! Sit down, Smiler. I was only kiddin'," Tranter hastily assured him.

Smith snorted but sat down again. Sat gazing abstractedly into the dancing flames that licked as the greasewood in the fireplace. But presently, as the clop-clop of nearing horses drifted to them through the cold clear night, he roused and turned his chair to face the doorway. Tranter got up and did likewise.

The hoofbeats slowed to a halt in the yard before the house. Come a creaking of saddle leather and several thuds as booted feet hit earth. With a jingle of spur chains the booted feet clumped across the veranda noisily. Then came a knocking on the door and Smith growled:

"Come in."

The door pushed open and Bast, followed immediately by Dixon and Two-Word Brux, entered. Brux closed the door.

With a sardonic grin Smith rose from his chair. "Ha! the Three Horsemen! Faith, Hope, an' Charity! Come right in gents an' tuck your little toes beneath the festal board!"

"Is that supposed to be funny?" Bast scowled. "You're playin' around with dynamite, fella, an' yuh better watch out. If it wasn't that we want to do what's right by you, we wouldn't have ridden over here tonight. I'm offerin' you your last change to get outa this mess peaceable."

"That's right friendly of yuh," Smith said. "What'll yuh have to drink, gents?"

Bast waved the proffered courtesy aside. "We didn't come to swill likker; we came on business. We'll give you ten thousand bucks for this run-down wreck of a place, an' five thousand more to clear out of the country an' stay out."

"Seems like your figgers is a mite low."

"They won't be as high again."

"No," Smith sighed dolefully, "I reckon not. But I don't

43

guess I'll sell just the same, though I thank you mighty much for the friendly offer. Yuh see, I've got sort of attached to this here ol' wreck of a place—I like the green grass an' shady trees an' the brook that babbles down the center of the valley. I been tryin' tuh think of a name to give that stream. How would Basty Brook or Big Al Crick do? It's sorta dark an' roily."

Bast's thick-lipped mouth twitched viciously. Jud Dixon gasped. Brux grunted:

"Damn fool!"

But Tranter chuckled. "Big Al Crick is aces high with me."

"Smith, you're a fool if you try to buck us," Bast snarled. "You can't lick a syndicate all by your lonesome. We got money, power, an' the law back of us!"

"Well, you ain't gettin' his ranch," Smith said flatly. "I won't sell an' I won't be driven out. I'm here to stick, so make up your minds to it."

"Mouth wash!" Bast sneered. "Either you'll sell out to us, or you'll soon wish yuh had."

"Is that a threat, Mister!"

"No, I don't waste time makin' threats. Its a fact; I'm talkin' cold turkey."

"I hope you gents ain't forgot the Tonto fracas over in Arizona," Smith said.

"What's that got to do with us?" demanded Dixon, scowling.

"I dunno. The government finally stepped in over there. I was just wonderin'."

"Humph!" Bast snorted. "The gov'ment won't step in here; it'll be wound up too fast. By the time the news gets out, this here fight'll be all over."

"An' we'll have the Smithers place, lock, stock, an' barrel!" added Dixon.

"Countin' your chickens, ain't yuh!" Smith grinned.

"We ain't countin' on nothin' we can't accomplish."

"Well, hop to it, gents," Smith said. "I ain't sellin' an' that's final."

The Big Three glowered. Bast's hand flashed down to his gun.

"Hold everything, gents!"

Crouched forward, staring wickedly through slitted eyes, was Tranter, gun in hand. His lips were tight-pinched lines beneath his squat nose. His body seemed tense as a coiled spring. "The boss don't care fer gun-play."

"Gawd!" Brux gasped. "Some draw!"

Dixon swore. "A gun fighter an' we never knowed it!"

"So you've hired that scurvy, rustlin' Tranter, have yuh?" Bast snarled, glaring at Smith as he removed his hand from the vicinity of his holstered weapon. "He was workin' for us till we caught him hidin' out a couple of our steers. He'll steal every danged cow yuh buy, Smith!"

"Oh, I reckon not," Smith appeared quite unruffled by Bast's attempted gunplay. Nor did Bast's accusation of Tranter appear to bother him greatly. "An' by the way, if I had stock in the syndicate like you three got, I'd sort of leave the fences of the S-Bar-S alone."

"S-Bar-S?" Dixon looked surprised. "Where is the S-Bar-S?"

"Right here," a sold grin curled Smith's saturnine lips. "I done give this outfit a new name."

"Well, it's all right with us," Bast said. "But why the crack about your fences?"

"I got three carloads of sheep on the way to Bucksnort. They'll be there in two-three days. I'm goin' to stock this ranch with sheep."

"Sheep!"

"Woolies!"

"Well, damn your soul!" swore Bast, his features livid. "You can't get away with that around here!"

Smith shrugged. "Stick around a while, fella, an' you'll find there's an uncommon lot I can get away with, once my mind gets made up."

"I'll stick all right, an' don't think diff'rent. I'll still be here after you're gone." He planted his barrel-stave legs well apart, hunched his massive shoulders forward and his pale piggish eyes flared with venom: "Before I get through with you, Smith, you'll be headed for hell on a shutter!"

"Tchk, Tchk, Tchk!" clucked the Smiler sardonically. "The vindictiveness of you fellas is shore amazin'. It ain't decent! 'Vengeance is mine, sayeth the Lord,'" he quoted solemnly. "Why can't we all live here in peace an' amity?"

"Vinegarones an' rattlesnakes ain't never mixed successfully with sheep," Tranter chuckled.

"You keep your car outa this," Dixon snapped. "An' put that fool gun away before the damn thing goes off."

"If it goes off it will be yore funeral, not mine," said Tranter pleasantly.

"Now listen, gents," said Smith in a conciliatory tone. "We don't want to carry this enmity of ours too far. It ain't decent an' it ain't healthy, an' the Good Book says there shall be 'Peace on Earth'. They can't be no peace if you fellas starts a range war.

"Now I'm all for peace, speakin' personal. I'm jest a friendly jasper what wants to love my neighbors an' raise sheep in peace an' plenty. I don't wanta stop my ranchin' every ten minutes to snatch up a gun an' blow some misguided jasper's brains out. It ain't Christian! Besides which, range wars is bad for the constitution, bad for the nervous system, bad for weak hearts, an' damn bad for busness! Let's love each other an' let bygones stay gone."

"Horsefeathers!" Bast sneered nastily. "Just another gust of wind! You can't bluff us outa this spread, hombre. We want it, an' we're goin' to get it!"

"Bluff? Mister, I've played a right smart amount of poker in my time an' I've learned one lesson well. It don't never pay tuh bluff unless yuh got enough cards to stand bein' called. Now, as regards this here range war we been talkin' about. I got the cards—you gents can call if yuh think you can stand the gaff."

"We're gonna call, all right," Bast said unpleasantly. "The first thing we're gonna do, is to make you prove the bill of sale you got for this place ain't been forged. An' if anyone asked me, I'd say it has. When the troopers hung ol' Smithers, the state confiscated this place. There's no record of a sale on the books. Your paper is signed by a fella named Crane an' there ain't no mention of the state. I aim to learn who this Crane jasper is—if there's any such a man! An' if there ain't, we sure got you where we want you!"

Smith ran a brown, lean-fingered hand through his yellow hair, tugged at his short mustache. This ornery Bast, Smith reflected, meant just what he said. And what he'd said was bad, only the Smiler knew. But it was pretty certain that Bast would find out before very long if he started an investigation. It began to look as though Smiling Smith had got himself in a tight spot, he told himself, and the tight spot was beginning to pinch! He straightened his gaunt form, grinned.

"Well," he said, with no apparent perturbation, "you gents can do as you see fit. I'm all fed up with arguin'. Crane is Crane, an' Crane sold me this place. If he forgot to record his own transaction with the state, I don't reckon there's much harm done so long as he's got the deed. I'll drop him a line about it."

"I'll drop him one myself," said Bast. "What's his address?"

"That's somethin' for you to find out durin' the course of your investigation," Smith replied. "Don't expect no help from me."

"Humph! If there is a Crane, I'll find him. Personally, I think you faked that bill of sale. What's more, I aim to prove it."

"Well, have a good, time," Smith grinned. "After you get all through fussin' around an' threatenin' peaceful fellers an' everything, I'll still be runnin' the Smithers place."

For a long ten minutes after Bast and his partners had

left, Smith stood in gloomy silence beside the fireplace, staring abstractedly into its dancing flames.

Finally Tranter could stand the strained hush no longer. "What's wrong, Smiler?"

Smiling Smith rubbed his lean hard jaw reflectively. "I ain't exactly sure, Buck, but I think Bast has got us in a forked stick this time. That damn bill-o'-sale business!"

"What's the matter with your bill-o'-sale? Did yuh fake it, like he said?"

"No," a bleak sort of humor shone from the Smiler's eyes, "I didn't fake it. I got it from this Crane jasper like I told him. But if Crane didn't record his ownership when he bought it from the state, we're sure gonna be sittin' atop one tall stump, an' no mistake."

Tranter shook his shaggy head. "I dont see it that way. If Crane bought it from the state, he's got a deed to it—"

"Yeah, I seen the deed, but forgot to get it from Crane. Hell, I supposed he'd recorded his title an' all; so I didn't think it necessary to get the deed after I realized I'd forgot it. I simply recorded my own purchase of the spread, never dreamin' he mighta forgot to record his."

"Well, I can't see what yuh worryin' about," Tranter said.

"Well, you will: I don't know how or where to get in touch with Crane! I don't know him from Adam's off-ox, except by sight!"

"You don't!" Tranter was astonished. "How did yuh come to buy a ranch off a stranger, I'd admire to know?"

"About a month ago," said Smith, "I had occasion to take a long ride on the Santa Fe. Some fellas an' myself was playin' cards in the smoker. After the game broke up, me an' another gent got sort of chummy. Nice fella, that Crane.

"Durin' the course of our talk, which of course was about cattle, sheep, range, an' so forth, he mentioned that he owned a ranch near Bucksnort which had been confiscated several years ago by the state. Wall, he was wearin' a badge of some sort, so I took him at his word, him bein' such a likable gent. The more he talked about his ranch— this one—the more interested in it I got. I asked him finally what he'd take for it since he said he didn't have time to do no ranchin', an' he offered to sell it to me cheap.

"I had some money I got for breakin' up the Wheatley gang, an' not bein' able to imagine a better use for it, I bought this ranch—the Smithers place. He made out a bill of sale an' got a couple of the other gents to sign as witnesses.

"Well, I had to get off at the next stop an' it wasn't till after I'd done so that I remembered I'd forgot to get the deed an' didn't know this Crane's address. Well, it was too late then to do anythin' about it, so I consoled myself with the thought that it probably wouldn't make any difference since I had the bill of sale, an' if he thought about it he could mail the deed to me here at the Smithers place. I ain't seen the deed, yet, though."

"Yeah," said Tranter sarcastically. "Talk about your suckers! He sure played you to a fare-the-well! What a shorn lamb you turned out tuh be, Smiler!"

"Aw, no. Crane's all right. He's a sheriff or a U.S. Marshal, or somethin'. Shucks, I'd swear he's straight as a die."

"It ain't goin' to make no difference to you whether he is or ain't—not now," Tranter pointed out with fine sarcasm. "If Bast don't find him quick the Big Three is goin' to swaller this here S-Bar-S of yours quicker'n you can wink!"

"Not while I'm in my right mind, they won't," Smith disagreed.

CHAPTER VI

MAYOR OF EL PASO

THE Smiler and his hired man adjourned to the kitchen.

"—yes, sir! An' the flossiest skirt this side of Dallas," Monahan was saying as they entered.

Smith stopped just inside the door. He planted his booted feet wide apart, his lips closed grimly as his hard eyes roved from the girl to the dude and back again. Dolores' cheeks were flushed and there was a sparkle in her eyes. She seemed to have been about to laugh whn Smith appeared. But now her laugh choked off.

There was a bold grin on Monahan's lips and a light of mischief in his mocking glance. The unexpected appearance of his host did not disturb him.

Smiling Smith stood rigid, the slow rise and fall of labored breathing giving his gaunt frame its only sign of animation. He did not return the other's smile, and his eyes on the detective's face were cold and flinty, hard with sudden menace.

Monahan turned to Tranter as though Smith's lack of answer, to him, meant less than nothing. "What you say to a game of cards?"

"Suits me, all right, if you got a hankerin' tuh lose some money," Tranter answered readily. "Let's go in by the fireplace."

Dolores lifted her eyes to Smith's when the two had gone.

"*Dios,*" she said, exasperation dripping from her tones, "ees that the way for keep the guest? Would you drive heem an' hees *pesos* from the *casa* for cast the eye at me?"

"Ain't you got no better sense than to flirt with a bird like him?" Smith demanded. "Don't do it again!"

"*That* for your ordairs!" her black eyes snapped with

scorn. "Do you theenk I am the *moza*, that you can tell me what I do an' what I not do?" Her cheeks were white with anger as she faced him.

Smith stood with grim lips parted, hard eyes on hers. "You'll do as I tell you by Gawd, or I'll know the reason why!" he said.

Her lips curled. "I do not have to stay here——"

Smith strode forward. Savagely he grabbed her by the shoulders, shook her. "No? Well, think again, sister. You'll stay here just as long as I tell you to, an' don't forget it. I'm the boss around here."

Dolores shrugged and turned away. For a moment there was complete silence in the room. Then, as Smith started to leave, Dolores whirled and darted to him, stopped him with her hand.

"Please, your honor——I am sorry for make you mad." With a sob in her voice she sped from the room.

For a long time the Smiler stood there where she had left him, and he was not smiling. The place seemed strangely empty for her absence. He could not understand what she had done to him.

When Smiling Smith entered the sitting room, the men broke up their card game. Not deliberately, but as though it no longer held the power to hold their interest. They looked at Smith and found him thoughtful.

"I couldn't help overhearin' some of the hot air them visitors of yours was spoutin' around here a while back," Monahan announced, abruptly. "Think they're pretty tough, I'd say from listenin' to 'em broadcast. What do you say, Smith, to a little private talk?"

"I don't have talks that can't include my foreman."

The detective looked at Tranter and grinned. "Foreman, cook, an' crew all rolled in one, eh? . . . Heck, I don't mind him! Let him stay if he wants.

"What I got to say may take some time," he went on. "I'd like to give you some advice, Smith."

"Advice? Well, go ahead an' get it off your chest. If I

get tired of listenin' I'll let yuh know."

"What about that bill-of-sale them birds was mentionin'?" the man from El Paso asked. "Anything wrong with it, or were they just hopin' there is?"

"That bill of sale is plumb bonyfied."

"Got the deed for this place, too? Or just the bill of sale?" The detective's glance was sharp.

"When you figgerin' to get the advice part of your palaver?" Smith asked.

"Soon's I get things straight in my mind. I can't advise you till I know your trouble, can I?"

"Humph! Well, I ain't got the deed, but I've seen it. It looks all right to me."

For a time Monahan was silent, pondering Smith's replies, one stubby-fingered hand caressing the hump of his broken nose, a far-away light in his jade-green eyes. Abruptly, he spoke:

"This Bucksnort banker," he said. "I've seen him before. He's got a past. Got another name, too. Used to live in El Paso when I was a dick there. When he pulled out one night, a lot of folks got headaches tryin' to figure where he went."

Smith and Tranter showed interest. "You talkin' about Si Jones?" Smith asked.

"Yeah. Only the name he went under in The Pass was Jalnor—Dan Jalnor. He was mayor."

"Jones? Jones was mayor of El Paso?" Smith looked astounded, and indeed he was. "Was he mayor when he left?" and, at the other's nod, "What happened?"

"Well, some officials discovered about a week later that a lot of kale had turned up missin'. City funds."

Tranter whistled softly. "The dirty skunk," he said.

"El Paso folks called him worse'n that, an' didn't give a damn who heard 'em," Monahan chuckled. "Jalnor was a slick 'un, all right. Maybe I better give yuh the whole story; you'll get the picture better.

"Jones, or Jalnor, was born an' raised in El Paso. His

folks were retired ranchers from the Panhandle. Always had plenty of money from all I been able to find out. About seventeen years ago, Jalnor was elected mayor by an overwhelmin' majority. After he'd been in office about four months he began sparkin' a high-toned Mex gal, a daughter of Don Anastacio Escobar—*juez* at C. Juarez."

"I wanta know," said Tranter.

"Yeah, the daughter of a Mex judge," said Monahan with a knowing grin. "Folks around town didn't hardly get wise to it though, till after he skipped out. Still, I don't guess he'd have hauled his freight if it hadn't been that opposition party was hittin' pretty loud that city funds was bein' misused an' demandin' an investigation. He'd been fillin' his pockets all right, an' knew damn well he couldn't stand no pokin' around by nosey dicks."

"Pulled out in the middle of the night, did he?" asked Tranter, grinning.

"Yeah, he pulled the pin in a hurry. Didn't even wait to say farewell to his *senorita*. She had a kid about six months after he skipped out. She's dead, now—been dead a good eight years."

"Where's the kid?" Smith's voice was thoughtful. "With the judge?"

"Nobody knows—but our ex-mayor is your Banker Jones, all right. I'll take my oath on that."

"How come he didn't recognize yuh?" Smith asked curiously.

"I was just a plain flat-foot at that time. I didn't get to be a dick till after Jalnor left. No reason why he should recognize me, that I can see. Now, here's where the advice comes in.

"To counter the threatened investigation of your lawful right to this ranch," Monahan said, "what you ought to do, Smith, is to get on your horse in the mornin' an' take a ride to town. Stop in to see Jones an' sorta ask him how he'd like a paid trip to El Paso. I reason that if you use your conk sufficient you can make a deal with Mr. Jones."

"Durned ef I don't think the dude is right," said Tranter, chuckling.

"Of course I'm right," Monahan grinned. "I'm always right."

CHAPTER VII

COLD TURKEY

BRIGHT and early the next morning, before Old Sol blinked the sleep from his eyes, the S-Bar-S was up and about. Dolores threw together some eggs, a batch of biscuit, beef and warmed-up beans which Monahan claimed was fit for kings—or the Mayor of El Paso, himself.

The dude guest was on his best behavior this morning. Not once did Smith catch him eyeing the cook. He seemed to have become aware of the fact that flirting with Dolores was not only tabu, but was a highly dangerous pastime— while Smiling Smith was around.

As soon as the breakfast things were cleared away, the Smiler announced that he was going to town. He seemed filled with that defiant spirit of adventure that had fired the hardy souls of pioneers and frontiersmen since the Dawn of Time.

As Sol's bright face crept above the saw-toothed horizon to the east, Smith mounted on Flea-Bite and with the roan's reins tied to Flea-Bite's bushy tail, Smiling Smith began his trip to Bucksnort. Tight-fisted Si Jones should be put in his proper place; the swashbuckling Big Three should learn that this grinning stranger in their land was a man of brain as well as brawn.

The morning still was youthful when Smith arrived in Bucksnort. Yet despite the early hour a very medley of sounds smote the eager ears of this gunless horseman. The droning of insects— chiefly flies of one sort or another. The rumble of passing wagons, large and small, heavy and light. The soft clup-clup of horse hoofs. A babel of voices —soft, gruff, pleading and challenging, masculine and feminine. The musical note of a hammer smiting iron upon an anvil in a nearby smithy.

The Smiler sighed. Just so would the world go on and on, even if and after the range-hogging Big Three syndicate succeeded in removing him from this sunny vale of tears.

In the very midst of these philosophic mismusings, the Smiler's attention was violently arrested by a sudden sharp jerk at his arm. Looking down from his advantage in the saddle he beheld the grim upturned face of a black-garbed stranger. The man was neither tall nor short. He had a slim waist and sinewy figure. His black clothes were threadbare, though of excellent make, and here and there about his person shone bits of glinting metal. Staring at the man's upturned features, Smith beheld a deeply-tanned face with gray eyes, sandy hair, firm mouth.

"Are you that Smith fella? The one they call the Smiler?" he demanded.

Smith nodded sober-faced, alert and ready for what might come.

"Fine," said the man. "I hear you're aimin' to do a bit o' hirin'. That right?"

"That's right," Smith answered. "You lookin' for work or wages, pardner?"

The stranger grinned good-naturedly. "Wal, a bit o' both, I reckon. I'm knowed as 'Trigger' Willmoth. If you can give me a job, I'd be obliged."

"Hmmm!" Smith studied the man appraisingly. "Trigger, eh? Sounds a bit gunnish, Willmoth. I'm figgerin' to run a peaceful spread, d'you see?"

"Peaceful, eh?" An odd twinkle gleamed momentarily in the puckered gray eyes of the black-garbed man. It was a twinkle strangely reminiscent of that in Smith's own gaze.

Smith chuckled. "All right, Willmoth, you're hired. When a man goes to work for me I never ask him no personal questions; I do my judgin' from his actions while he's with me. Light out for the ranch now an' report to Buck Tranter. He's foreman. Tell him I said to put yuh on."

Smith turned his horses toward the Kallis stable.

Banker Si Jones, sorting the litter of papers on his polished desk, looked up abruptly as his office door clicked open and grimaced wrily at sight of his unwelcome visitor. "You back again?" he scowled. "I told you last time I wasn't makin' no loans on the Smithers place. I ain't see no reason to change my mind since you was in here yesterday."

A cold grin curled the Smiler's saturnine lips. "I reckon not. Howsomever, I didn't come to borrow money. I come to have a talk with you."

"A—a talk?" the banker faltered, suddenly suspicious. "I don't see what you an' me can have to talk about, Smith."

"You will," Smith told him ominously.

Jones shivered slightly. This grinning stranger was a tough proposition, he reflected nervously. It might be best to humor him. "I'm always willing to listen," he hastened to assure.

"You better be. I ain't minded to take no slack jaw from you this mornin'. I come here to talk about the valley I bought—the Smithers valley. That bunch of hard-shelled land-hawgs are doin' their damndest to run me out. Knowin' that you're a sorta silent partner in the syndicate, an' backin' it financially, I figgered you was the best man to come to terms with."

"Terms?" Si Jones took sudden courage at the familiar word. He knew all about terms, and how to always work them out to his advantage. Terms! It was a ray of sunshine in the cloudiness of Smith's presence.

The narrowed eyes with which the Smiler studied the banker grew slowly dark and ominous. Si Jones wanted to look away and tried to, but could not. Gazing fascinated by a stronger will into the outlander's glinting eyes Jones read death. This Smith had killed—there was at this moment the look of a killer in his glassy stare. Deep down within him the banker shivered. The ray of hope aroused by the outlander's mention of terms vanished, and left in its wake no sign of its passing unless it was the marked paleness of the banker's features.

"How'd you like to take a trip, Mister Jones?" There was sardonic laughter on his lips as Smith added: "A trip to El Paso?"

To Si Jones his comfortable office seemed suddenly cold —cold with a penetrating chill that pierced his bones. Its picture-hung paneled walls seemed to be drawing away from him, diminishing in the distance and leaving him cold and alone to face this demon with the grinning lips. Stark dread shone from his tiny eyes. Dread of Smith. Dread of this thing he sugested.

"What—what do you mean?" he said and did not know his voice.

"Just that. A trip to El Paso. I reckon the folks down there would welcome their old friend, Mayor Jalnor, with open arms. Don't you?"

Jones' face went pale as ashes; his mouth sagged, twitching, twitching.

For a long time neither spoke. The silence grew tense and brittle—cold. A well-built office was this room of Banker Jones; no sound from the outside world came into disturb its occupants. And just now no sounds were heard within it, save the ticking of a clock and the rasp of the banker's breath.

When the first shock of the Smiler's revelation wore away, the shaken banker began to wonder where his outlander had obtained his information. Had he come from El Paso? Had he come to take its ex-mayor back? Or had that dude—Yes! it must have been the dude. The fellow had made no secret of whence he came. Yes, surely the man had recognized him somehow and had passed his recognition on to Smith. How much did Smith know? . . . How much had the stranger confided?

"What—what is it you want of me?"

"I want to make a deal," Smith said. "I want you to stop the big syndicate outfit from rakin' up any trouble about my bill of sale for the Smithers place."

"An' in exchange you'll agree to keep your mouth shut?"

"I'm not makin' any promises. But I can tell you this much: If the Big Three force my hand on that bill of sale business, I'll take it out on you."

The banker's chill had passed. "What's the matter with that paper? Ain't it any good? Ain't there any gent named Crane?"

"Such questions as you're askin' is bad for the health, Jones—your health."

"But if Crane really sold you that place, an' it was his to sell, all you got to do to prove it is to produce this fella Crane."

"That's all," said Smith. "An' I will, if necessary. But I don't want to bother him unless it's vital."

"Well, I'll see what I can do about stoppin' Bast—"

"You better do your best," the Smiler told him ominously, and closed the door.

Again, as on a not-too-distant former occasion, four scowling men sat in the private office of the Cowman's Bank of Bucksnort. The icy silence was portentous. The Big Three stared unblinking at their silent banking partner. Jones shivered, and cleared his throat.

"It's hell, I reckon, but we got to face it. What are we goin' to do now that Smith has got me in a tight?"

"I'll tell yuh what we ought to do," snarled Big Al Bast. "We ought to go right ahead with our plans an' if he's got somethin' on yuh, let yuh take your medicine! It's hell of a note the Big Three had tuh pick a crook for their pardner!"

The banker's face went purple. "You better watch out, Al Bast," Jones' voice was thick with anger, "who you're slingin' names at. There's two or three names I could put to you that wouldn't sound so nice!"

"Gentlemen! *Gentlemen!*" Brux gasped in quick alarm. *"Please!"*

"That fella, Smith, is a slick one," Dixon said thoughtfully. "He's going to take some handlin'. In case you fellas ain't woke up to the fact, he's the gent who cleaned up on the Wheatley gang! He's a ring-tailed roarer when he gets started. We don't want to rile him much until we're ready to settle his account."

Jones' eyes popped open at mention of the once-dreaded Wheatleys. Bast growled deep in his throat and clenched his ham-like fists. Brux looked hastily about, as though fearing Smith might suddenly materialize.

"Just what is it Smith has got on you, Si?" Dixon asked abruptly.

"None of your damned business!" the banker snarled. He dared not reveal his true identity to these men, for he knew his partners would sell him out if they ever got a chance. "Never you mind what he's got on me; we got to lay off that bill of sale an' that's all there is to it!"

"I ain't so sure of that, Si," Dixon's eyes were thoughtful. "I believe we can get around him if he doesn't know too much. You think it's this dude that tipped him off?"

"I don't know who tipped him off. But the dude sure strengthens his hand," he reluctantly admitted. "What you got in mind Jud?"

Jud Dixon's bronzed, hard-chiseled features reflected thought—thought and purpose, too. There was a determined light in his bright-button eyes. "I was thinkin' mebbe this dude could be bribed to swap sides," he said

But what he *thought* was a little different. Jud Dixon was the type of man who not only looked ahead, but was oftentimes able to turn what seemed defeat to positive advantage. He believed that this was such a time. If Monahan had tipped Smith off to something in Jones' past strong enough to force the banker to come to terms, Jud Dixon wanted to know what that something was. It might, he thought, be something he could use himself in bringing his tight-fisted partner to heel.

The other three looked at each other a bit uneasily. Bast spoke their common thought: "If the dude will swap sides once, what's to stop him from swappin' back to Smiths' side again later?"

"Nothin'," said Dixon, without revealing his private intentions. "That's a chance we got to take. Ed Kallis said he was a detective. Mebbe he can detect somethin' in Smith's past to our advantage." He paused a moment to let this sink in firmly, then concluded:

"Smith will be back in a day or two to find out if we're droppin' that threatened investigation. You tell him, Jones, we are."

Presently Bast again entered the conversation. "Did yuh notice what a gunslinger that Tranter's turned out tuh be? We gotta stop his clock quick. We gotta stop them damn sheep, too!"

"Sheep!" Jones snapped. "What sheep?"

"Smith is figgerin' to stock the Smithers place with sheep," Dixon's voice was soft. "If he does, we may as well give up all hopes of ever usin' that valley again. It'll take years to get the sheep-stink of that range once Smith puts woolies on it."

But it wasn't the prospect of sheep in Smithers valley that was bothering Dixon. It was the problem of getting a clear title to the valley for himself that was stirring the rancher's thoughts to action. Dixon wanted that valley and its ranch headquarters, not for the syndicate but for himself. There was something there he meant to get. And he didn't aim to share it with these men who were his partners. Certainly, he told himself grimly, not while he was in his right mind.

"Well, you needn't worry about them blattin' woolies," Bast grinned. "I'm figgerin' to take care of them personal-like. They'll never spoil the grass of the S-Bar-S!"

Back at the Smithers place, Smith's captivating house-keeper was busying herself about the kitchen. Tranter and the dude guest were playing casino in the sitting room or on the porch for a nickel a point. Dolores wasn't sure whether they were in the house or on the veranda, and didn't much care. The more she saw of Monahan, the less she liked him. He was, she fancied, a lady-killer, and though she craved attention from the stronger sex, she had no use for the type of attention that was Monahan's stock in trade.

What Dolores wanted was attention from Smiling Smith. He was the breeze she set her cap to catch. Each time he came near her, her being quickened. A most romantic figure, she thought this grinning, gunless *gringo*. He stood out in bold relief against the horizon of her thoughts, and she longed for his attention—for his love. She wanted it as she had never wanted anything in all her wanting life.

He was slim and strong and clean. She knew it, for her judgment of men was acute; made so by experiences grim and heartless crowded into her small span of years. Eight years on her own along the border country had quickened her perceptions, sharpened her wits and made of her what she was—a lovable, wistful waif; plaything of Destiny.

Small wonder that in Smiling Smith she saw a champion of the oppressed, a righter of wrongs who did not stop to weigh the odds. She loved him whole-heartedly for what he was himself; for his recklessness and daring, for his swashbuckling disregard of consequences.

If he would only love her just a little, it was all she asked of the gods.

She looked up as a shadow darkened the doorway. The dude dick stood lounging against the frame, his bright green gaze admiring, a cynical smile on his curling lips.

"I suppose time hangs heavy on you around a place like

this, don't it?" he asked, letting his gaze rove about her supple form admiringly. "It's a wonder to me that you stay here."

"I am happy just to be here, *señor*. Nowhere else could I be the one-half so satisfy. Do you not like eet here?"

"Oh, it suits me all right. I wouldn't want to stay here very long, though."

"Perhaps the food, she does not agree weeth your honor? Too much Mexicana, maybee?"

"Oh, the food's all right—I like spicy things," he said suggestively, and chuckled. "How about takin' a little ride with me, *mi querida dulce?*"

Lowered lashes screened her dusky eyes.

"At least, *querida,* you will give me a little kiss, eh? Just one?" his hard grin revealed a flash of teeth. He was proud of these teeth; they had captivated many women.

"I am not your sweetheart," Dolores protested. "An' my keeses belong to *Señor* Smeeth."

"That clod!" Monahan snorted. "Hell, he don't even know enough to come in when it rains! Come on, now— pucker, darlin'."

There was a light in his eyes she did not like, nor did she care for the flashing teeth revealed by his curling lips. She began to back away as he started for her. He moved forward, eyes aflame. He caught her to him. Hot color stained her cheeks. There was cold fury in her tawny eyes as she struggled to get at the knife inside her bodice.

He strained to crush her to him and this hot breath fanned her face. Curses tumbled from her carmen childish lips; low they were, and filled with panting hate. Then suddenly she felt him stiffen. With a snarl, he thrust her from him.

Buck Tranter was lounging in the doorway. There was a grin on his lips but it was not pleasant. Nor was there anything pleasant to be found in the way his gnarled right hand dropped by the thumb from his belt, a scant half inch from his gun. Cold words drawled from his parted lips:

"That ain't included in your eighty bucks a week."

CHAPTER VIII

"LADIES DON'T ACT THAT WAY!"

IT was late afternoon and Old Sol was preparing to go to bed when the Smiler came jogging back to the S-Bar-S. Buck Tranter was taking his ease on the veranda, his chair tilted back, his feet on the railing and his battered old pipe between his grinning lips. The dude detective was not in evidence, but Smith saw Willmoth lounging on the bunkhouse steps.

Stripping his gear from Flea-Bite, Smith turned the animal into the pole corral and, nodding to Willmoth, strode toward the veranda. From the open kitchen door came a merry, appetizing rattle of divers pots and pans. And on the same air current that brought these interesting sounds to Smith from out the kitchen, was wafted a multi- tude of aromas which caused the Smiler to wrinkle his nose with anticipation.

"Wall," hailed Tranter, as the boss of the S-Bar-S paused before him, "has anything worth relatin' happened in Bucksnort town today? Did yuh tie knots in the tails of any of its important citizens?"

"I sure laid down the law tuh Banker Jones," Smith chuckled. "The fear o' Gawd is in him now an' I reckon he's about to see the error of his ways. He actually shivered!"

"Now, that's what I'd call 'good listening',". Tranter grinned. "Has he agreed tuh stop the syndicate from carryin' out that threat?"

"He said he'd do his best."

"Humph!" Tranter snorted. "I can tell yuh right now it won't be good enough!"

Smith chuckled, in no manner worried about Si Jones. He might not have chuckled, though, had Tranter told him of the dude's adventure in the kitchen. But the lanky foreman kept that incident to himself.

When Dolores had cleared the supper things away, Tranter caught Willmoth's eye and winked. "What do you say to a game o' poker, Trigger? A friendly game for table stakes. . . . Somethin' tells me Yeller-Shoes feels in a mood fer cards. We gotta entertain him if it's possible, yuh know. This here's a dude ranch an' we gotta help tuh make it pay."

Tranter and Willmoth rose from the table. "I'd jest as soon play a few hands," said the latter. "I allus been curious tuh see how these here city fellas play. Did yuh ever hear, Buck, what happened to that dude over at 'Pache Ike's what said somebody had cheated him?"

"They took him out an' hung him," Tranter's face expressed regret. "I hope there won't be no call fer such measures tonight. It would be kinda tough on the boss if we had tuh hang his only guest."

Monahan scowled as he shoved back his chair. "All right, wise guys," he muttered, "I hope tuh hell I take everything but your breath away!"

"We'll play in the bunkhouse," Tranter said, and grinned.

After they had gone, Smith picked up the ledger he had bought in town that afternoon and went into the sitting room, After a glance at its bright new pages, he flopped into his cowhide chair beside the fire and began entering figures in the debit column. It was not a task to his liking.

Dolores came in as it was getting dark and lighted the kerosene lamps. Without speaking she returned to her kitchen chores. Presently Smith heard her singing softly.

He soon flung down the ledger in disgust and put the pencil stub he'd been figuring with back in his shirt pocket.

His three carloads of sheep should arrive at Bucksnort some time tomorrow. He reflected that he'd have to ride in and make arrangements for having them driven to Smithers Valley. He should have thought of it while in town today. He was getting thoughtless as an old hen, he told himself.

For a moment his reflections focused themselves on Buck Tranter, gent of easy conscience and rider of the ready iron. There was scant doubt but what the man was a rustler, Smith thought. Still Tranter had the look of a man with whom a gent could ride the river.

Trigger Willmoth also held the look of a reliable hand. Still, a man could never tell. Faces were mighty deceitful things. Willmoth's puckered gray eyes were deep. For all Smith knew, Willmoth might be a syndicate spy. He decided it would pay to keep his eyes open.

He did not care two whoops in the hot place for his dude guest. But the man was a source of revenue and, for that reason if no other, must be tolerated.

That he was bound to have further trouble with Black Potak, the syndicate foreman, Smith realized well. The fellow was not the type to forgive a pistol-whipping administered with his own weapons.

As he sat there, gazing into the fire, Smith wondered who and where the man Crane was. It was a pity he did not know where to look for the star-toter. He had an idea that if he could find the man, many of his present difficulties would be ironed out.

Uncommonly odd it seemed that the syndicate should be taking so much trouble to get him off this property. Surely they were not going to all this bother merely because he had taken a goodly chunk of their range from circulation? Could it be that there were wheels within wheels to this plot to force him from the country?

Dolores was still singing in the kitchen. It was getting on his nerves. He called her. When she came, he said:

"Is that necessary?"

She looked a question.

"That singin'," Smith grunted.

"It does not please your honor?"

"I ain't crazy about it," he admitted.

"Perhaps you would rather have me make the loff—"

"Can you read?"

"But, yes—"

"That's it!" he growled. "You been readin' too many of them durned love stories! That's what ails you—all the time talkin' about love. It's enough to drive a fella batty! Yuh got to cut it out. There's limits to my endurance, gal!"

"Eef I had not tol' the sheriff you were in loff weeth me, where would you be—"

"There yuh go! Throwin' that up in my face again. Gosh—"

"For shame, *señor!*" her dark eyes flashed. "I'm theenk I go somewhere else to live."

In three quick strides he crossed the room, grabbed her by the arms. "Yeah?"

"Or maybe I weel flirt weeth the *Señor* Monahan—"

"I'll warm the back of your lap if I catch yuh at it!" Smith growled angrily. Just because he didn't go in for this love stuff himself was no reason why that damn dude should profit by Dolores' presence. He'd be darned if he was going to stand around and see someone else loving his bewitching housekeeper. If he didn't care for this love stuff himself, there was going to be no loving done on the S-Bar-S!

She shook free of his grip, twin spots of glowing color in her olive cheeks.

"Be your age," Smith growled, "an' quit talkin' about this love stuff! Try bein' a lady for a change." He paused to summon his thoughts, then added:

"You go around makin' sheep's eyes at me half the day. Yuh've got tuh stop it. Ladies don't act that way!"

"This is what-you-call the 'leap-year'. Besides, I am no

lady. An' do not weesh to be one. An' what ees more, I'm theenk a lady would die of the old age waiting for the *Señor* Smeeth!" •

Smith glowered.

"Don't you loff me even tiny beet? Just a little?"

When several moments of silence had passed, long-drawn breathless moments during which it seemed to the girl Smith made no least attempt to answer, the color faded from her face.

She shrugged abruptly; a salute to hopes and dreams that were no more. Her scarlet lips curled unpleasantly, a bitter, metallic burst of sound. Her dark eyes flashed contempt for this yellow-haired gringo who did not care for love.

"I will go, then," she turned away, and there was moisture in her eyes, tears that she would not let him see.

But he caught her, whirled her round and saw them. And, seeing them, did a thing that even he had not thought possible—he kissed her; square and true upon the lips.

CHAPTER IX

TWO-FISTED WARRIOR

WHEN Smiling Smith got up from the breakfast table next morning and clumped his gaunt frame down to the corral, Buck Tranter strode along after him. When the Smiler slapped his saddle on Flea-Bite, the foreman spoke:

"Goin' tuh town again today?"

Smith nodded.

"What fer?"

"It ain't none of your business, but I'm goin' to see if I can find somebody tuh drive my sheep out here. They oughta be in town today."

Arms akimbo, Smith's ragged foreman stared reprovingly at his boss. "What you need is a guardian, boy. Ain't you got no better sense than tuh go rompin' in to Buck-snort every day? Why, you'll wake up one of these mornin's with a hunk of Big Three lead sailin' through the crown of yer hat!"

Smith grinned. "Shucks," he said, and climbed aboard his nag.

"I'm plumb serious, Smiler. You're takin' one gosh-awful risk ridin' that trail reg'lar. Bast or Potak'll lay fer yuh one one of these bright mornin's. How about me goin' with yuh?"

"Not on your tintype!"

"Why not?"

" 'Cause this mornin', Buck, I want you to go out an' check up on our fences. See that they're in condition; take a look at the range, the water-holes an' so forth. Take all day. I'm goin' to have those sheep out here in a coupla days—"

"Yeah, an' that's just the reason you ought not tuh go gamblin' into town alone. It ain't only the Big Three; ev-ery two-bit rancher in this country'll be after your hide when they learn you're aimin' to bring sheep in here! Heck, Smiler, this is cattle country! Folks around here look on sheepmen like they do on foreigners—the only good 'uns—in their notion—is dead 'uns! Think it over!"

"Applesauce!" jeered Smith, and feeding Flea-Bite the spurs, left his foreman standing in a cloud of dust.

"All right, you durn young know-it-all," growled Tran-ter. "But don't never let it be said I didn't warn yuh!"

Smith swung down from the saddle before the hitching rail outside the Cowman's Bank. After tethering Flea-Bite, Smith cuffed his shabby old Stetson to a rakish angle and went striding into Si Jones' institution with a saddle-bound swagger.

As he passed down the small and narrow lobby, clerks looked up and, seeing who the newcomer was, looked hastily away again.

Si Jones peered at his visitor with a sober face, his beady eyes half-closed.

"I was thinging mebbe you'd left the country, Smith."

"Where'd yuh gather in that loco notion? Why should I pull out?"

"Well," Jones said pointedly, "there's other climates that would probably be better for your health."

"Nothin' the matter with *my* health, Mister. I like this country fine; there's more crooked jaspers bedded down around here than any place I ever been—outside a penitentiary! Makes me feel right to home, so to speak. I'm a sort of badman-buster by trade, you know."

"It wouldn't surprise me much if your badman-bustin' days are about over, young fellow," the banker said portentously. "There's two or three gents in this locality that would be right glad to see your hide nailed to their barn doors."

"I reckon they're due to be disappointed then," Smith grinned. "Get any action on that little matter we was talkin' over yesterday?"

"Yeah." The banker's skinny hands were cutting slender strips from his desk blotter with a pen-knife. "The Big Three have decided not to push that investigation."

"That's right-down nice of 'em. Glad to see they're showin' good judgement. Well, I guess I'll be siftin' along. It's gettin' close to grub time an' I got a lot of things to see to. Take care of yourself, Mister Jones—don't go out without your overshoes."

Leaving the bank, Smith emerged into the bright sunlight streaming from the pale blue of the cloudless heavens. It was hot—durned hot, he thought, and decided to get a drink to wash the alkali out of his throat. He turned his steps toward the Tall Bottle saloon.

But at that moment, having come almost to the steps of the saloon, Smith stopped short. For a man had just pushed open the swinging doors and emerged to come to a sudden stop halfway down the steps. He was a man with a Navajo headband about his forehead, and a tiny black mustache on the upper lip of his swarthy handsome face.

"Howdy, Potak," the Smiler grinned. "I been wantin' to see you about a little matter—that money you borrowed off me a while back."

A malignant scowl twisted the syndicate foreman's face. "Money, eh? I guess you're referrin' to the money you claim yuh left on Ed Kallis' desk?"

"Right first pop outa the barrel," said Smith, ignoring the foreman's scowl and the manner in which Potak's hands had dropped to rest on the twin cartridge belts encircling his hips. "Bein' a little short, I reckon I'll have to recall that loan, as the bankers always tell yuh."

Potak threw back his head in an ugly laugh. "Well, recall be damned," he said. "Since you're so good at quotin' proverbs an' sanctimonious sayin's mabbe you heard the one that goes: 'The Lord helps them that help themselves'?"

"Yeah, I heard that one," Smith started up the steps, reaching into his pocket for tobacco and papers as he did so.

"Don't be in a hurry," Potak's deep voice was omnious. "I want to see you about a matter, too. An' this is a right good time."

Smith poured a sprinkling of Durham into a rice paper cupped between the fingers of his left hand, put the sack back in his shirt pocket. "Yeah?" he asked, and stopped on the step below the syndicate man. "You referrin to that pistol-whippin' I gave yuh?"

"You guessed it!" snarled Potak, and brought his left gun up in a flashing arc that swept straight for the Smiler's head.

Rice paper and tobacco spilled from the two-fisted cowpoke's hands as he jerked his head backward; caught the arm whose hand held the flashing gun in a grip of steel. Came a blur of motion and there was Potak sailing over Smith's left shoulder in a flying mare.

The Smiler was on him before Potak could pick himself out of the dust. But the syndicate foreman was hard as iron rails and just now was a raging fury. He lashed out with swinging fists, kicking, swearing, snarling. One flying foot caught Smith in the thigh, sent him reelng backward to fall at the foot of the steps.

Both men came to their feet together, dust-covered, red of face and breathing fast.

With a bellow of rage, Potak charged. His right hand lashed out in a vicious haymaker. But the Smiler leaned backward and the blow went short, whirling Potak half around. Smith lifted a booted foot—dust flew from the gunman's pants.

When Potak picked himself from the ground the second time, his swarthy face was twitching with baffled rage, hoarse oaths were tumbling from his snarling lips. One hand reached down to his boot, came up with a heavy knife. With glaring, slitted eyes he circled the Smiler warily, abruptly rushed, knife raised.

Smith's left arm blocked the blow. His right swung out like a striking snake. Flush on the jaw it caught the dark-faced man and Potak's head snapped back and he went over backward to lay sprawled prostrate and motionless in the dusty street.

Rubbing his aching knuckles, Smith stooped above the fallen foreman. From Potak's pocket he drew a purse, opened it and extracted several banknotes which he placed in his own chaps pocket. Then, retrieving one of the scattered cigarette papers from the steps of the Tall Bottle, Smith scrawled a receipt, placed it in the purse and returned the purse to Potak's pocket. Then he grinned.

"I reckon there's one badman that'll be plumb good for fifteen or twenty minutes," he chuckled, and turning, he started up the saloon steps. "It'll be uncommon odd if folks around these diggin's don't learn pretty soon that pickin' on Smilin' Smith is a right painful sort of a pastime!"

He paused outside the swinging doors. "Funny nobody came out tuh see the fight," he muttered. "I wonder if there was any special reason why they didn't?"

Pushing open the doors he entered the resort, and then he knew. He was just in time to catch the tail-end of a conversation that, to him, all but spelled disaster:

"—Cl'ar off the track at the Big Bend trestle. Freight cars, flat cars, sheep cars, engine an' all. An' brother! when they hit them rocks at the bottom of the gulch yuh could of gathered the remains of them damn woolies in a bushel basket!"

Smith was stunned. At that moment a feather would have pushed him over! There was no doubt in his mind whatever as to whose sheep were being discussed. He was the only man in the county who would have dared to bring sheep onto the Bucksnort range. He realized now how damnably he'd overplayed his hand the other night in telling Bast and his partners about those sheep he was expecting. He did not doubt that Bast had been behind the wreck at Big Bend trestle—Bast was the man of action for the syndicate forces; Bast's was the hand that had dealt him this blow beneath the belt!

Then suddenly the hair at the back of Smith's neck began to prickle. Only now did he realize why these men in the Tall Bottle had not emerged to watch the fight! The Smiler jerked awake with a surge of anger. As he glanced around through slitted lids, the muscles along his lean jaw tightened. He had stepped into a trap—and the trap was about to spring!

Crouched in advantageous position about the long room stood a ring of sinisterly silent men; men with grinning faces and gloating eyes that were filled with triumph. Outside the swinging doors behind his back, Smith caught the sound of stealthy feet crossing the loose boards of the porch and knew in that flashing moment that there could be no retreat.

Smith's mouth lost its grin, snapped to a tight vivid line

of white, and his frosty eyes behind their slitted lids held cold blue flames of anger. With taut face and hard-clenched fists he eyed the crouched and silent men about him. Bast and his gunhawk crew represented a formidable fighting force; but Bast and his six were up against an Arizona whirlwind.

"Clear the trail!" Smith shouted and, like a cat reversing ends, he spun around, seized a chair as he whirled and dropped flat as the Big Three crew reached hipward. A blast of gunfire that shook the flimsy building roared above Smith's prostrate figure, tearing jagged splinters from the door. Though their reverberations lingered, the weapons of the Big Three faction went silent as abruptly as they had flamed into action.

"Figgered they got me, damn 'em!" Smith thought. Beyond the doors he could hear the gurgling sobs of a man in agony and the sound of another thrashing about on the porch outside.

Through the drifting powder-smoke he could see the gunmen milling.

With the chair still clutched in his upthrust hands, the speed-blurred figure of Smiling Smith surged to its feet and went dashing in among them. Right and left Smith swung the chair. Men went down beneath its deadly circles like wheat before a scythe. Shouts and groans, sobs and curses swelled and rumbled to a very pandemonium. A scattering of frantic shots broke out, futile at the speed the Smiler moved as he whirled among them, ducking, dodging, smashing.

"A new kinda mash, polecats!" he jeered. "Come an' get it!"

A syndicate man leveled his smoking weapon at the Smiler's back as the cowpoke momentarily paused to catch his breath. Before he could pull the trigger one of his companions, dodging through the smoke haze, caromed into him and sent him sprawling. Their very numbers told against them.

Jeering and mocking Smith zig-zagged among them creating havoc, striking and dodging, constantly on the move, never giving back an inch but ever on the aggressive, carrying the battle to Bast's men. His chair was demolished to kindling wood and he flung the last splinter aside and dashed among them bare-handed, striking, smiting, laughing.

A man beside Smith reeled and Smith caught him in his arms, swung him aloft and hurled him among his companions, mowing several down. Smith roared his battle cry and charged once more among them. It was his only chance and he knew it. If he ever let himself be outlined in the clear, a score of bullets would send him down like a broken twig.

Dodging a flying bottle that someone let drive from the bar, the waddy from S-Bar-S ducked head first into a floating chair. He went down headlong to the tune of splintering wood. But he wouldn't stay there. He came lurching to his feet somehow, shook himself free of the remaining debris and again got into motion, weaving, stumbling, straining his red blurred vison nto the dusky reeling mists that swirled before him. His split lips parted in a sobbing breath: "Play cards, Smiler! Don't quit till the last chip's been swept away!"

The revolvers of the syndicate men were, to themselves, worse than useless and they suddenly began to realize it. They did not dare shoot while that crazy yellow-haired fool from the S-Bar-S, like a wildcat with a knot tied in its tail, was weaving his erractic course back and forth among them. Once or twice after that first blast they had tried using their weapons, but swift howls from one another of their number had soon convinced them that Smith must be downed by hand.

A faint draft abruptly cut through the haze of smoke that swirled about the barroom. Smith's aching ears caught the swift trip-hammer crash of a rapidly exploding gun from the doorway back of him, and he guessed its wielder instantly. Black Potak was fanning desperately for revenge. The searing bite of lead ripped past his ribs like a white-iron. A leaden hornet sang through his hair. The whine and zip, the crash of breaking things and the startled yells of the syndicate men in the line of Potak's fire was all about him. But Smith refused to drop.

"Don't quit till the last chip's gone!" Again and again the words dashed through his mind.

His left shoulder abruptly shrank beneath a gun-barrel and the Smiler went sagging to his knees. The man who struck, Black Potak, let out a howl of glee.

"I got the damn, slab-sided, sheep-herder—that time!" he yelled above the uproar.

"You're daffy as a gopher!" Smith whispered through battered, bloody lips that hardly moved. With a mighty effort he got upon his feet. There was something warm and sticky running down his face. He wondered what it was. Then he saw a face in the murk before him, and it was the face of Big Al Bast. He lashed out at it. He must have scored a hit for the face disappeared, he thought. But he felt no pain, nor heard no sound save a curious roaring in his ears. Then, strangely, everything went black.

CHAPTER X

ONLY A SAMPLE

A DEEP strange voice that seemed somehow familiar despite its strangeness, brought Smith back to consciousness. The air was redolent of alcohol and horse liniment. With an effort Smith opened his eyes and found himself lying on a couch, his movements more or less restricted by divers bandages large and small. A big fellow with a ferocious black mustache with upturned ends was bending over him, shaking him with a huge pawlike hand. Upon this big man's vest gleamed a heavy metal star.

Sheriff Dan Hellman scowled. "What the hell you been tryin' to do around here, young fella? You dang near wrecked the Tall Bottle!"

Sitting up, though somewhat dizzily to be sure, the Smiler rubbed his craggy jaw. "I been tryin'," he said sardonically, "tuh keep soul an' body the way the Lord intended."

The Bucksnort lawman's beefy face broke into a grin and his eyes grew bright and twinkled as he regarded the battered young buckaroo before him. "Son," he said, in a low sort of voice, "I don't often butt in on the syndicate's affairs, as yuh've likely figgered out for yourself. But they was makin' such a hellemonious racket playin' tag with you over in the Tall Bottle, I just felt like I'd better amble over.

"Danged lucky I did, too. 'Cause there was you goin' down for the final count, d'ye see? Then I sez to myself, sez I, 'There's a young fella what's right smart of a man. It wouldn't be right to let them buzzards stop his clock.' So I steps in, d'ye see?"

"I'm obliged to yuh, sheriff. Did I do much damage?"

"Damage? Wal, I dunno. Damage is a sort of multitudinous word," Hellman grinned. "I mean it covers consid'rable territory. Ye sore busted, mangled, maimed an' otherwise hurter in divers and sundry ways about the six best men on Bast's payroll. Then there was three fellas more or less shot up. Smith, you been near enough tuh hell to smell the sulpher an' brimstone. But I reckon I can't hold ye for that."

Smith looked around. He found that he was sitting on an old dilapidated couch in the sheriff's office. It was a small room and rather scantily furnished. There was a great smear of reward notices thumbtacked to its walls.

For a time Sheriff Hellman was quiet, apparently thinking, then abruptly he spoke once more:

"I'd like to give ye a piece of friendly advice, Smith. I recognize it ain't good manners an' I imagine you're a man that'll go his ways regardless——"

"That's all right," Smith chuckled. "I'm always ready to cock an ear to good advice, even though I don't always foller it. Shoot!"

"Wal, it's this: The Big Three jest about own this county. They usually manage to get their way when they want anything. They been usin' your range for the last four-five years free an' without askin' any gent's permission. You come along an' buy that whole valley. The big Three, countin' on continued use of that range, have overstocked. The minute you fence it they find they're up ag'in a scarcity of fodder. They either got to sell a passel of stuff dirt cheap, or get more range, or watch their cowbrutes wizzle away from lack of eatin'.

"Put yourself in their position. What would you do? I'll tell yuh: You'd try to do jest what they're tryin' to do—take Smithers Valley by hook or crook, An, they'll do it, too. Legal if they can. But if you crowd 'em they'll resort to less gentle measure. I can't help yuh, Smith, so if you stay you'll have to fight 'em without the law's protection. I couldn't get a posse around here without it was made up of Big Three men an' Big Three sympathizers!

"My advice tuh you, young fella, is to climb aboard your flea-bit nag an' take a nice long ride clear outa this country. What you jest got was only a sample of what you'll get if you hang around Smithers Valley."

"Yeah? Well, what I give them fellas in the Tall Bottle was only a sample of what Smilin' Smith can do, too!" the S-Bar-S boss scowled. "I'm stickin—come Bast, hell or plain high water." Smith spoke the last sentence without heat, threat or bluster. He spoke it as a simple statement of fact. The sheriff accepted it as such.

"I figgered ye would," he said, and nodded. "Wal, ye better be gettin' home an' gettin' some rest. You're shore goin' to need it!"

From the sheriff's office Smiling Smith betook his bandaged self once again to the Cowman's Bank. Jones grinned when he saw the patches the Smiler's hide was sporting.

"Looks like you been up against a buzz saw, Smith."

"No," said Smith, "I was shavin' with a new razor an' it slipped a mite. It won't happen again, though, so don't look so darn hopeful."

"Have a drink?" asked Jones, and pulled a bottle from a desk drawer. Smith nodded, so they tossed one off and Smith felt considerably better. "Why don't you give up the Smithers place, Smith," the banker asked. "You'll be savin' yourself a lot of trouble."

"Shucks, trouble an' me's old bunkies," the Smiler chuckled. "Besides, I'm too set an' stubborn-like. Bast is startin' tuh push things now, an' I never did like gettin' pushed. Nope, I reckon I'll play out my string. I jest dropped in, Jones, to tell yuh that if anything more happens to me or mine, the Big Three had better do some fast movin'. I'll be goin' now—sweet dreams."

The banker shivered involuntarily as the S-Bar-S man backed out the office door.

Outside the bank, Smith recollected the matter of his slaughtered sheep. He started for the door again, then changed his mind. It would do no good to talk to Jones about those sheep the Big Three had derailed at Big Bend Trestle. He couldn't prove, conclusively, that the Big Three had even had a hand in the affair, though of course he knew they had.

With a weary shrug, for he was bruised and tired and patched in a dozen places, Smiling Smith climbed into the saddle and at a slow jog, started for home.

Twenty minutes after Smith left town, another conference was staged in the private office of the Cowman's Bank in Bucksnort with Si Jones presiding.

Dixon laughed. "We sure got that Smith maverick on the run, now," he chuckled.

"Run, hell!" Brux snorted.

Jones looked curiously at the man who never used three words where two would do. "He looked pretty patched an' feeble to me," he said thoughtfully, his skinny hands again busy with the pen-knife. "What makes you think we ain't got him on the run?"

"Ask Bast."

The other two looked at Big Al, who scowled. "If you think Smith was patched up," he grunted grimly, "you oughta seen my men. Cripes! they look like they been through the Battle of Bunky Hill That damn Smith's a wildcat if I ever seen one!"

"I hear Potak was doin' some shootin'," said Jud Dixon, pointedly. "Why didn't he stop the Smiler's clock?"

"He would have, all right, if that ory-eyed Hellman hadn't come bustin' in at the primest moment. Smith knocked hell outa Potak just before the fracas started in the Tall Bottle, an' when Potak come to he was all primed tuh do some butcherin'. That's the trouble with pickin' a dumb but honest man fer sheriff; we should uh knowed better!"

"Humph! Dan Hellman better walk the chalk line if he expects to hold that office after next election," Jones snarled. "We put him in office, an' by gosh we can put him out!"

"Unless Smith wins," Dixon's tone was thoughtful. "In that case, if Hellman don't side with us too plainly, the Smith faction will vote him in again."

"Did you stop his sheep from gettin' here?" Jones asked.

Bast guffawed. "Did we stop 'em? Hell, there ain't enough of them woolies left tuh make a decent stew of!"

"We got to hit Smith again, an' we got to hit him quick an' hard," Dixon's tone was definite, his harsh mouth and bright-button eyes held a look of determined purpose. "The loss of them sheep musta put quite a crimp in his pocketbook. If we strike again before he can recuperate, he's done. What about them fences?"

"It's an idea," Bast admitted, "that I been thinkin'

about. I'll tend to 'em tonight. But here's somethin' you're overlookin': Takin' down Smith's fences will annoy him, like enough, but won't hurt his pocketbook any to speak of. 'Cause why? 'Cause he ain't got no stock to keep inside the fences anyhow, so he likely won't bother puttin' 'em up again right quick."

"Oh, yes he will," Dixon differed. "He won't want us to go drivin' our stock outa his valley! If he puts 'em up, it'll cost him money."

"He can get money from that dude guest he's got visitin' him," Bast growled. "I seen that ad of his in a paper the other day. That dude is payin' eighty bucks a week. That's a lot of money in a month. That's—"

"Nothin' for you gents to worry your heads over," Dixon cut in with a grim smile. "I had a talk with that dude this mornin. I think I can get him to leave Smith's without much trouble whenever we want him to. In the meantime, it might be useful to have him stay there. He might overhear somethin' that would benefit us."

"Fine," Jones rubbed his skinny hands. "You got a real head on your shoulders, Jud."

Dixon looked at him and grinned; not an over-pleasant grin, either. "You bet," he said cryptically. "I plan to think of most things a little bit ahead of the next gent—that's the way tuh be successful."

As Smiling Smith, patched and not in the best of spirits, jogged along the trail to Smithers Valley, humped over in the saddle like a bent pin, he thought of many things. Chief among them, Dolores.

In the language of the border cow country, Dolo of the scarlet rags was a girl of courage. She had backbone and grit, tenacity, too; qualities the Smiler could admire. He found himself wondering who her parents had been and if they had been residents of Bucksnort. He wondered where she had got the little gold locket which she wore on the thread-like golden chain about her neck.

He wondered about that kiss he had given her the night before, and about the way her scarlet, childlike lips had clung to his, and the way her arms had crept about his neck.

He wondered, also, what he would do for stock, now that Bast had derailed his three carloads of sheep—sheep that were not completely paid for.

He mused over his recent fracas with Black Potak, the syndicate foreman, and wondered what new deviltry the fellow would think up to get even for the loss of prestige inflicted on him when the Smiler had publicly bested him before the Tall Bottle Saloon. And he wondered also at his almost miraculous escape from what seemed certain death during that rumpus with Bast's men inside the drink emporium.

Was this, after all, the end of his gallant plans for the S-Bar-S? Was this the end of his hopes to put his newly-acquired property once again on a paying basis, as it had been during the five-year reign of Smithers?

The Smiler's wide shoulders slumped as he jogged along the sandy trail through the bad lands of the Devil's Boot. It began to look, he told himself lugubriously, as if the Big Three with Jones' financial backing were going to prove too much for him. Smiling Smith began to wonder if, after all, he had not bitten off too big a mouthful in going up against the biggest outfit on the Bucksnort range.

Then abruptly he snorted. "Play cards, Smiler!" he admonished himself. "Don't never throw in your hand till the last chip is swept away!"

One man, if determined enough and backed by a couple of gun-slinging hellions like Tranter and Trigger Willmoth, might accomplish much if he set his mind to it. And though he could not count on any help from Sheriff Dan Hellman, the lawman had sort of hinted that he needn't worry over-much about being bothered by county law. Plainly, it was up to Smiling Smith to play his hand.

And equally plain was the hint that he needn't play strictly according to Mr. Hoyle!

So, in a somewhat more cheerful frame of mind, the Smiler pushed his Flea-Bite horse in a slightly faster gait over the dusty miles that lay between himself and Smithers Valley.

When Smith came in sight of the S-Bar-S, the afternoon was well nigh spent; the sun was inking low above the west rim of Smithers Valley. It was a tired and dusty Smiler that stripped the saddle from Flea-Bite's back and turning him into the pole corral, strode stiltedly toward the house.

Monahan was sitting on the veranda, feet atop the rail, a black cigar between his unsmiling lips. He regarded Smith through half-closed eyes.

"What happened to you? Get run over by a mowin' machine, or somethin'?"

"Naw," said Smith with a sour grin. "I been kissin' a bull, as the fella said. Where's Willmoth? Tranter got back yet?"

"Willmoth's in the bunkhouse takin' a nap, I guess. I ain't seen Tranter since I got up."

"What time was that?"

"Oh, I dunno. 'Bout twelve-thirty or one o'clock."

"We serve three meals a day on this outfitt," Smith said bluntly. "Them as don't appear at table durin' them times don't eat. Remember that hereafter. I won't have Dolores workin' all day jest so you can lay in bed. This ain't no sanitarium."

"Okay by me," Monahan yawned. "Where's all them sheep I read about in your ad? I ain't seen a dawgone one since I been here. Where d'ye keep 'em?"

"Them sheep you read about in the ads has been delayed by condition of the rails. Yuh'll have tuh lay their nonappearance onto the A. T. & S. F."

"What's the matter with the rails?"

"Somebody pulled 'em up," Smith said, and went in the house.

CHAPTER XI

Villainy Afoot

THE ranch headquarters of the Big Three syndicate were an imposing array of log buildings sprawled in a sheltered clearing on Crawling Dog Crick, some half dozen miles from Smithers Valley. The cook shacks, barns, sheds and the great log bunkhouse were situated in a great circle about the log ranch house. The latter, though not of adobe, was constructed in the Spanish manner. Carved *vigas,* hand tooled beams, projecting on both sides formed the roof for a wide and shady veranda floored with red Spanish tile. Here the Big Three were wont to sit and sip their whiskey-and-sodas during the long hot afternoons, or sit and smoke their pipes and expensive cigars in the cool of the evening.

Before the entrance that led off the front veranda of the great log house, four ancient pepper trees reared their trunks and drooping fluid branches gracefully. These trees were the especial pride of Two-Word Brux, who would sit for long hours dozing in their shade. The creekside was a green line of live oaks and big-boled cottonwoods that were the envy of ranchers for miles around.

But with all their fine headquarters and good range-land, the Big Three coveted and meant to have the range where Smith had settled. For years they had fattened their cattle there in summer on the fine lush grasses that had cost them not a penny. They saw no reason why they should not do so now. The matter of Smith's having spent good money to acquire this property meant little or nothing to Bast, Dixon and Brux. Smith had no business buying something that the Big Three had long considered their undisputed own. Smith should have had better sense than to buy land sight unseen. Since he had, it was up to him to sell or take the consequences. He would not sell so the Big Three proposed to make the consequences drastic. No matter what the cost, this stubborn outlander must be removed!

Sitting smoking on their cool veranda as the setting sun was sinking below the horizon of the bad lands, the Big Three were talking over the fiasco of that afternoon's affair at the Tall Bottle.

Abruptly raising his hand, Brux pointed out across the tumbled chaos of rock and sand that was the Devil's Boot. "Company comin'," he announced.

His companions leaned forward in their chairs the better to scan the terrain in the direction indicated by their taciturn partner.

"Looks like that damn dude that's stayin' at the Smithers place," Bast growled. "What the hell's he doin' comin' over here. He's got his guts."

"When I was soundin' him out this mornin' I asked him to ride over tonight," Dixon's soft tones gave answer. "I'm kinda interested in knowin' just what he's got on Si Jones. Might be somethin' we could use. Si's been skimmin' the cream off our profits for a deal longer than I like to think about. It's time we did somethin' about it."

"Yeah, he sorta stole a march on us that time he bought up so much of our floatin' stock. There oughta be a law against that," Bast said testily.

Brux sat silent, his fishy protuberant eyes watching the approach of the distant, awkward horseman.

"Smith sure made a monkey outa Potak this afternoon," Bast growled after a time. "Potak had his gun out an' Smith just picked him right up and flung him over his shoulder. Cripes! that guy's strong as a bull-moose! I never see his beat."

"Tough jasper," said Brux, succinct as usual.

"He's tough an' he's lucky. But his luck can't hold out

for ever. We'll have the skids under him in a week or two, or send him to hell on a shutter." Dixon puffed thoughtfully a while, then rapped his pipe against the veranda railing. "That girl of his, now—that raggedy baggage he picked up in Bucksnort. We might be able to get him through her."

"That's a real idee," Bast approved instantly. "We'll kidnap her an' make him come to terms."

"Kidnappin's out," Brux scowled. "Too dangerous."

Dixon nodded. "The country wouldn't stand for it. We don't want to decorate no damn cottonwood limbs—leastways, I don't."

"Me, neither."

"There's other ways," Bast growled deep in his bull throat. Dixon had unleashed a new line of thought for him and he meant to track it to its various possibilities. "This girl notion is a damn good idea, seems to me, an' ought to be worth a bit of thought. There's likely some way or other we could handle that filly without gettin' into trouble over it."

Nodding slowly, as though he agreed that there might be, Dixon chuckled to himself. If Bast was damned fool enough to go get himself in trouble over Smith's ragged housekeeper, why then that was Bast's own fault. And if he got himself strung up by a bunch of wrathful cowmen, well then that was one less with whom the syndicate profits must hereinafter be divided.

Potak, too, thought Dixon shrewdly, might offer possibilities in connection with the girl. It all depended, of course, on whether or not the Smiler really cared for her. But, anyway, it was worth considering. Many a man, he knew, had been got at through a petticoat!

Presently Monahan, having arrived within hailing distance, let out a whoop. The Big Three raised their hands in careless salute. "Let me do the talkin' with this dude," Dixon muttered, and rose to greet the newcomer as he drew rein before the pepper trees and climbed stiffly from the saddle.

Fifty yards away, a puncher sitting against the bunk-house wall, shifted the rifle he was holding so that its muzzle centered in the proximity of the third silver button on Monahan's purple shirt.

"Come up on the veranda an' make yourself to home," Dixon invited. "Pretty hot, ain't it?"

"Well, I'd call it cooler here than back in the burg I come from," Monahan said, mopping his face as he sank into Dixon's vacated chair. "Many's the time I've seen it a hundred-an'-twenty in El Paso. What did you wanta see me about, Dixon? Let's get to business."

"I guess mebbe we'd better," Dixon's bronzed, hard-chiseled face was expressionless. "We're going to be rather busy around here tonight, an' I guess you're anxious to get back to the Smithers place. You an' I can likely talk a deal better in private. Let's go sit in my office."

"Suits me," Monahan rose and followed his host inside.

Seated in the luxurious ranch office of the Big Three, with a glass of "whiskey-and" on the table beside him, Monahan glanced inquiringly at the man across the table, wondering just how much this visit could be worth to him.

"The reason I invited you over tonight, Monahan, was to learn what it is you have on my partner Jones, the Bucksnort banker."

"What makes you think I've got anything on him?" the dude countered warily.

"Smith came to town the other day an' threatened Si, but Si won't tell us what Smith held over him. It strikes me that whatever it is, it's somethin' that you brought up. What'll you take for passin' the same information on to me?"

Monahan lit a cigarette and thoughtfully blew smoke rings. Finally he stamped the cigarette out with a knowing smile. "About two hundred bucks will buy that info you're after, Mr. Dixon."

"Hell, I ain't no gold mine, fella. Act your age."

"Two hundred bucks is the price, Mister."

"It ain't worth that much."

"You're the best judge of that, I guess." Monahan's eyes were bright and hard.

"This is robbery," growled Dixon, peeling two hundred dollars off his personal bank roll. "It's like handin' you a Christmas present."

"Well, I ain't askin' you to do it, you know. It's your suggestion. After all, this information is worth a whole lot more than I'm askin' for it."

Dixon snorted. "If it was, you would be askin' more."

"No, I can't collect on it, myself." Monahan put the money the other handed him carefully in his pocket, leaned back in his chair and grinned.

"I told Smith," he said, "that Jones was an embezzler."

"Was he?" Dixon's tone was soft and thoughtful. There was a calculating light in the glance he turned on Monahan. "Or was you kiddin' Smith?"

"No, I wasn't kiddin' nobody. Jones is an embezzler— or was, a matter of some fifteen years ago. He skipped out with about—well, I ain't sure how much, but it was quite a bit."

"What was he, a bank cashier or something?"

"The answer to that will cost you another cool hundred," Monahan grinned.

"Say! what do you think this is? I paid you for the information you passed on to Smith an' I mean to get my money's worth."

"You got the dope I gave to Smith. If you want the names an' places an' dates an' all that stuff, it'll cost you more. I got quite a shock when I recognized Jones an' realized I couldn't cash in on my discovery. I passed this information on to Smith for nothin', like a damn fool. But if I pass it on again, I aim to be paid for it."

Dixon's mouth became a white grim line of anger. He passed the dude another banknote. "Open up, an' don't stop for breath. Three hundred bucks is all I'm payin. What was Jones, an' who was he?"

"Jones was Mayor Jalnor of El Paso. He skipped out one night with some city funds."

Dixon whistled softly. This *was* news! "Did the city offer a reward?"

"I don't guess they did. I don't guess they were anxious to advertise the deal. A lot of people got bad headaches though, tryin' to figure where he'd gone to."

"Is that all you told Smith?"

"Not quite. I told him that Jalnor had been foolin' around the daughter of a Mex judge over in Juarez," said Monahan, adding with a coarse chuckle: "They say the *senorita* had a kid after Jalnor skipped out."

Dixon thought over the dude's revelation. He certainly had a hold over the banker, now. But it was a hold shared with Smith. And further, it was nothing with which he could spike the guns of Smith—unless he and Bast and Brux were willing to sacrifice the banker. Well, after all, why not? Why not go right ahead with the investigation of Smith's bill of sale and title to the Smithers place and let Smith do whatever he wanted to in regard to banker Jones?

"That Tranter fella over at our place is a bad actor," Monahan murmured irrelevantly. "I'd find a way to get rid of him if I was you birds. He'll cause you trouble if you don't."

"Humph, what you got against Tranter?"

"Me? I ain't got nothin' against him," Monahan grinned. "But I overheard him talking with Smith about the possibilities of rustlin' some of your prime beef—"

"The hell you did!" Jud Dixon scowled, not knowing that Monahan was lying.

"Yeah," the dude tried a random shot in the dark: "Tranter was tellin' Smith how he'd pulled a few like deals for you fellas when he was workin' for the Big Three."

Dixon said nothing, but he did a lot of silent thinking with the resulting conclusion that Tranter would have to be removed speedily before he began talking elsewhere. His mouth must be shut once and for all.

"Well, I guess I'll be siftin' along. Don't want Smith to be gettin' nosey about where I been," Monahan chuckled as he got up. "I'm much obliged for the hand-out, Mister Dixon. Hope I can be of service again."

"You can," Dixon told him. "Just keep your ears skinned. If you hear anything we oughta know, ride over."

After Monahan had ridden off and Dixon had joined his partners on the veranda, Bast growled:

"What did that damn scissor bill have to say?"

"He was handin' me the low-down on Brother Jones— otherwise known as Ex-Mayor Jalnor of El Paso."

Several moments of startled silence followed Dixon's soft-spoken revelation. Bast, Brux and Dixon looked at each other thoughtfully and slowly grinned.

"Well," said Bast with a nasty laugh, "I guess that finishes Si Jones with this combine!"

"Just how?" asked Brux.

"Well, even with his slight majority of the Big Three stock, I don't reckon he'll be feelin' frisky enough to buck our plans while we hold that Ex-Mayor business over him."

"Beyond me," said Brux. "What's he done?"

"He embezzled some city funds and had to leave El Paso in a hurry," Dixon told him. "Now here's an idea I been thinking over, gents. If we go right ahead with our investigation of Smith's title to the Smither's place, he'll probably force Jones' hand. Jones will either have to skip out or get taken to jail or El Paso, if Smith can establish Jones' true identity. But—that ain't doin' us a mite of harm. In fact," Dixon grinned slowly, "no matter what Smith does about Jones, it will actually benefit us three."

"You're right," Brux nodded his hatted head emphatically. "Great idea."

"Well, you sure got a head on your shoulders, Jud," Bast grudgingly admitted. He puffed out his fat, black-stubbled cheeks and yawned. "Reckon it's about time to get the boys together and started on our little tour. Moon'll be up in another hour. Any of you fellas want to come along? Glad tuh have company, yuh know."

"Not me," Brux spoke hurriedly. "Too tired."

"I'd like to go, Al, but I'm goin' to be powerful busy this evenin' checkin up accounts an' all," Dixon seemed regretful.

Bast sneered. "You two pussyfooters give me a pain sometimes! You act like you're scared of your shadders! Cripes! that Smith jasper's only human—a bullet'll knock him down just like anyone else," and, grunting disgustedly, he bowlegged off the porch, spur chains jingling.

"How about the cattle?" Dixon called after him.

"Gonna let Potak an' a couple other jaspers start driftin' 'em over right now."

"What if Smith an' Tranter start rustlin' 'em? They'll have a damn good chance if we shove 'em over there."

"Just let 'em try," Bast sneered malevolently. "If we catch 'em at it, that Smith wrinkle of ourn will get ironed out plumb permanent!"

In the late afternoon of this same day Buck Tranter, on the second day of his fence-riding job, made camp in a broad ravine out by shallow brush-filled washes. This place, the only one where S-Bar-S and Big 3 territory touched, was known by the arresting title of Grasshopper Draw.

There was reason in Tranter selecting this spot for his camp site—good reason. The wily ex-rustler knew very well that sooner or later the syndicate was due to start something. When they did get down to business, if they decided to stage a raid on the S-Bar-S, they would have to approach by way of Grasshopper Draw; said Draw being the only southern entrance to Smithers Valley.

Just as the sun slid down against the western horizon, Tranter might have been seen crouched above his tiny camp-fire, skillet in hand, frying flapjacks for self and pony, the latter watching each expert toss of the drying batter with anxious eye.

As soon as their meal was over and Tranter had emptied a second battered tin cup of coffee, washed the dishes in the spring-fed headwaters of Crawling Dog Crick, he rolled up in his blankets and steered at the winking-blinking stars, which seemed but a scant rope's length above him.

After a time the moon, filled to bright yellow roundness, began its evening roll across the heavens. The desert night was quiet and peaceful, lovely in its silent way. The low pleasant chirping of the night insects droned in Tranter's ears, and the occasional restless movement of his picketed horse, which he had left with saddle on.

The moon as it rose higher in its orbit washed the broken outlines of the valley's southern rim with silver; was reflected in the gurgling stream. From a scant distance, Tranter could hear the steady *crop-cropping* of his grazing horse, and the lazy muffled plopping as it slowly moved among the mesquite clumps.

Then abruptly the ears of the dozing puncher caught the sharp click of horse-shoes distantly striking stone.

Tranter stiffened in his blankets, suddenly threw them off and sprinted for his pony, who stood with rigid neck and perking ears gazing south. Swiftly the ragged puncher examined the saddle, drew the cinches tight. He pulled the picket pin and wound the rope, retrieved and rolled his blanket, lashed it behind the saddle and swung aboard his horse.

Then he waited.

Presently a line of black-garbed horsemen rode into the draw from its entrance on Big 3 territory. Reaching the wire fence strung by the S-Bar-S, several of the horsemen dismounted, stooped beside the tight-strung strands of wire.

Zing-g-g! Zing-g-g! Zang-g-g! The wires were down!

Cursing silently, Tranter yanked his rifle from the scabbard, cuddled it to his shoulder, squeezed its trigger with eager finger. The sharp report rocketed away across the range, rang and echoed against the distant valley rim. The dark-garbed group about the line fence scattered. Swiftly they got a horse, hauled long guns from saddle scabbards, rushed spurring for the lone guarder-of-the-fence who, with a last defiant shot, spurred his mount and fled before them.

Six hours later, a great herd of bawling white-faced cattle were driven into the southern entrance of Grasshopper Draw. With a laugh, Potak told his men:

"By noon these critters will be well into Smithers Valley, dinin' on the best damn grass in Bucksnort County! C'mon le's get home tuh breakfast—this won't be no place to linger in, come daylight!"

CHAPTER XII

WHEN THE MOON SHONE DIM

ON A lathered, blowing pony, Buck Tranter reached the headquarters of the S-Bar-S around 4 A.M. He flung himself from the reeling steed before the bunkhouse door and, almost before his booted feet hit dirt, Smiling Smith was standing in the doorway glaring. "Now, what the hell's gone haywire?"

"Bast an' his damned gun-hawks is cuttin' our fences!"

"Where?" Smith's tone was ominously calm, his narrowed eyes held a steely gleam.

"Grasshopper Draw, when I left. I flung some lead at 'em but had to clear out. There's too damn many of 'em for one man tuh tackle—even me! What the devil d'yuh figger they think tuh gain by cuttin' fences?"

"Probably aimin' tuh drive their white-faces onto our grass, I shouldn't wonder," Smith's lips twisted in a mirthless grin. "They got nerve enough, all right."

"Want I should saddle yore nag?"

"What for? I ain't goin no place. Neither are you. Yuh better turn in an' try an' get some sleep."

"Sleep!" Tranter exploded. *"Sleep!* What the lop-sided hell're you talkin' about?"

"Slumber—you heard right the first time, Buck?"

"Hell! ain't you gonna do nothin' about this?"

"Yeah—but not now. You leave it tuh me. The Big Three'll find it's a heap easier to get their cattle on this spread than it'll be tuh get 'em off! We'll let 'em feed here a while an' then I'll send Bast a bill for grazin'."

"Humph!" Tranter snorted. "That's a funny kinda remark for a fightin' he-man like you tuh make. Was it *my* grass what was ketchin' hell, I'd be out there shootin' steers inside of five minutes. Mebbe they ain't gonna drive—"

"Yeah, they'll shove their cattle on our grass, all right," Smith grinned. "But don't let it bother yuh, Buck. There'll be a diff'rent tune sung tomorrow. Turn in now an' get some rest. We're apt to be up all night."

Tranter hitched up his frazzled corduroy trousers and gave Smith a curious stare. Seemed to him like there must be a couple loose screws in the Smiler's cranium. First jasper the ex-rustler had ever known who blew hot one minute and cold as ice the next. Such a contradictory nature as Smith appeared to have kept a fellow guessing all the time. Damned unsatisfactory sort of a gent to work for, Tranter thought. Never could figure what he'd be up to next. He shoved back his floppy-brimmed sombrero and scratched his shaggy head.

"Yuh aim tuh let them mangy Big 3 jaspers eat up your grass right under our nose?" he demanded incredulously. "Why, they might even rip our fences down complete!"

"Always turn the other cheek's my motto, Buck. I can't do nothin' till they've slapped me on both sides. You're right about that wire, though. They'll raise the devil with that, all right. Part of their program—make things as expensive for me as possible. I might have tuh quit if they do enough damage. Leastways, I guess that's the way Bast figures it."

So saying, Smiling Smith with a saturnine chuckle proceeded to lay his gaunt frame once more on his pine-slat bunk in an earnest effort to woo again that elusive goddess —Sleep.

Promptly at noon the Smiler rose and, after splashing for some moments in the basin on the bench outside the kitchen door, sat down at table with Monahan, Tranter, Willmoth and the girl and ate a hearty dinner.

When they were filled to capacity, Tranter, Willmoth and the dude produced tobacco in various forms according to their separate taste and adjourned to the shade of the cool veranda for a spell of smoking. Smith surprised Dolores by helping her clear the table and stack the dishes beside the tub of water in the kitchen. Then he hunted up a flour sack and dried them as Dolores washed them.

After the dishes had been put away, Dolores came to her yellow-haired boss and held up her scarlet lips invitingly.

Smith looked them over in impersonal approval. "Not bad at all, kid. When you get two-three years older I don't doubt they'll be right temptin'. Yuh want to be more careful, though. Sometime you'll do that with some gent what ain't got a iron self-control like me, an' you'll get 'em kissed."

The girl's lovely childish lips curled into an adorable pout. She stamped a bare foot and the coins looped about her ankle jingled musically. "Perhaps," she said, giving him a reproachful look from half-veiled eyes, "that is what I weesh."

"Quien sabé, niña de los ojos—who knows, my darling of the lovely eyes?"

"Has your honor no feeling in hees heart?" her long-lashed eyes grew misty as she eyed him with mute appeal. "Am I so unlovely in your honor's eyes?"

"Yeah, I got feelin' all right," he answered, "an' you're pretty as a picture, *niña*. But I ain't very good at this durn love stuff. I'm a two-fisted hombre whose speed is on the hoof. I ain't had no time for practicin' these here parlor arts—"

"But I could show your honor—" she began hastily, moving closer.

"Well, yeah, I reckon yuh could. But not this afternoon," he added nervously as she clasped her golden arms about his neck. "I—I got a lot tuh do, right now. It's a heap important, *niña*."

She looked him in the eyes and the Smiler squirmed uneasily. "Ees there then something, perhaps, more eemportant than loff?" her tone was plaintive, adorably beseeching. "Could you loff me just a leetle first?"

"Whew!" Smith said to himself, and felt his face grow hot. What in sixty could a promising young cowpoke do with a housekeeper who acted thus? Seemed like all girls thought of nowadays was love! It was terrible, the way they carried on. He'd like to got his hands on that fellow who invented leap-year!

"There ain't a thing that I'd like better, Dolo," he said in what he hoped was a fervent tone of voice. "But I can't stop any longer now. I got a ton of work what's waitin' for my attention. I just gotta get it done! But tonight, mebbe, I'll let yuh show me how a gent should hold a lady's hand—how a gent should pant an' goggle. But, *right now*, I gotta work!"

The moon shone dim that night and all the world seemed fast asleep when three silent, shadowy figures stole from the bunkhouse on the S Bar S and softly flitted toward the corral, reached it and roped and saddled a bronc apiece with a noiselessness that was uncanny. From the desolate sandy wastes of the Devil's Boot a lobo's long-drawn howl to the silvery disk in the cloudy sky was heard as they rode away.

Their way took them along the course of Crawling Dog, Crick toward Grasshopper Draw. They came upon Big 3 white-faced cattle, three great herds of them which, on Smith's whispered oders, they skirted: "No sense startin' a stampede," he muttered. "That's good beef an' some-day it may be mine—a part of it, anyhow, in payment for my sheep."

It was an eery night. The dark sky was filled with scudding clouds that hid the moon from time to time and sent long shadows, dark and grim, across the broken range. The rhythmic cadence of muffled hoofs and the soft gurgling waters of the stream were the only sounds that broke the silence as they rode out the southern end of Grasshopper Draw, past snarled and slashed wire fences heading for the headquarters of the syndicate ranch. Even the insects seemed to have stilled their noc-turnal chorus. All the land seemed hushed and waiting.

It was a night of portent.

Back at the Smithers place as soon as he was sure Smith, Tranter and Willmoth had departed, Monahan slipped softly from his bunk, stole out the door even as had the others. But unlike them, he did not go near the corral. Instead he moved stealthily toward the adobe ranch house, where slept the Smiler's housekeeper, and there was a hard, calculating grin on his freckled, reddish face.

Cautiously he approached the kitchen door which he had learned by observation was seldom locked of nights. Reaching out he tried the knob. It was not locked tonight. His grin grew wider as softly he pushed the door open. It squeaked a bit and he waited tense and rigid. But noth-ing happened. He stepped inside.

As softly as was possible, step by step, he approached the closed door of Dolores' room. He must not awaken her; he brought a long, thin-bladed knife from his belt and inserted it in the crack between the door and its jamb, sought for and found the oaken bar the girl upon retiring had dropped in place. He got his knife blade under it and softly, slowly, cautiously raised it from its socket. Holding it so, he pushed the door ajar, then softly let the bar down.

Returning the knife to his belt, Monahan pushed the barrier inward, inch by stealthy inch. Slowly, then, he moved across the floor, pausing rigid and breathless each time a floorboard squeaked or groaned beneath his weight. It was a nerve-racking trip, that journey from the door to the girl's four-poster bed. But he made it. The devil's luck was with him.

A fugitive ray from the cloud-enshrouded moon stole through the open window and lay across the bed illuminating the sleeping girl's slight figure, the slow rise and fall of her rounded breasts, her childish lips and tender beauty. Her tawny locks lay tumbled about her piquant fact, her long-lashed eyes were closed.

Monahan's right hand stole toward her throat. . . .

In Bucksnort, Banker Jones was busy. A short time after ten, he had left his quarters and gone to the bank where he let himself in the back door, after hastily looking about to make sure he was not observed.

Inside his private office Jones lost no time in getting to work. There were a number of things, he felt, badly needing his immediate attention; things that might not be looked to during the routine of banking hours.

From time to time he glanced about him covertly and cocked his head to one side as though intently listening for some sound he failed to catch—some dreaded sound, if one were to judge by the expression in his beady eyes.

With nervous swiftness he fingered piles and stacks of

papers; some pink, some blue, some yellow and others plain white, but all bearing on their surfaces lines of ink-marked figures. He examined dusty files and divers documents which he took from book-like pasteboard boxes in his safe.

He worked with blinds drawn level with the sills. And there was an expectant sort of tension in his movements, a nervous tension born of fear.

He pored over ink-scrawled ledgers, his bird-like glance darting up and down the figured columns, his gimlet mouth tight-closed. And as he worked among his books and dusty papers he paused often to glance about with fearful stare.

These pauses came most frequently when visions came before him, mental visions that came between his eyes and the things at which he stared. There was one particularly potent—a grinning face with flinty, mocking eyes that jeered his hastening efforts; a grinning, taunting face that chuckled knowingly at his midnight labors. A face he wished he'd never seen—that of Smiling Smith.

There was another face that helped to heighten his uneasiness; soft and oval, piquant and framed in dusky hair wherein a rose was twined. A face whose brooding eyes had haunted him for eight long years, lovely, passionate yearning. It was that of the woman he'd left in C Juarez, across the Texas Border.

As these images came before his mental vision, Jones would snarl, panting vicious oaths and wiping the beaded moisture from his face with skinny, shaking hands. And sometimes these phantom masks would vanish for awhile. But the banker had no peace. Fear had too great a hold upon him, and premonition was reaching out its bony hands.

Suddenly a sound broke in upon the banker's work. A sound whose significance he was quick to grasp. A sound which caused him to remain motionless in his chair—the sound of an opening door.

"Looks like you're about to pull your picket pin an' do the El Paso on us, Si," the voice was familiar to the banker, but he did not change position. "Rather lucky I changed my plans—some I made last night—and decided to pay you a little visit. I had a notion you'd be here. Ain't you goin' to turn around and talk with your old friend?"

Jones held his rigid position in the chair beside his desk. His knees were shaking and the room felt cold to him—cold with the chill of a dank stone vault. His teeth would have chattered, but he dared not part his clenched jaws for fear of crying out.

"I was aimin' last night to put our plans through whether you liked it or not. The only thing you could do, had I done so, would not have hurt your associates in the slightest, like enough. But, thinking things over this afternoon, I decided you could do us a lot of good, maybe, if handled right. I'm here to handle you right tonight, Si. You won't have to hunt a new hole-up now, in order to keep your skinny carcass out of jail." An unpleasant chuckle broke from the speaker's harsh mouth. The bright-button eyes in his bronzed, hard-chiseled face glowed with sardonic humor.

"You're about to do your partners the best turn that is in your power, Jones—you're about to die."

Slowly, like a creaking automation, the banker turned. His face went pale as ashes. His eyes filled with horror as he saw the glint of metal in the speaker's hand, the blue-steel glint of the .45 that was leveled at his chest. . . .

Mounting streaks of orange flame blossomed simultaneously on the black night from three separate buildings at the Big 3 headquarters on Crawling Dog Crick. Swiftly the brightening flames ran up the bone-dry logs of the burning structures, lighting up the deserted clearing, throwing grotesque and wavering shadows across the uneven ground.

Abruptly oaths and shouts arose from the darkened bunkhouse where men awoke to the long-drawn howl of a lobo—awoke with smoke in their nostrils and the sound of burning wood crackling ominously in their ears.

Abruptly the bunkhouse door burst open, spewing its startled occupants onto the hard-packed ground of the clearing that was steadily growing brighter in the light of the leaping flames.

Sparks, carried by the chill night wind that drove great clouds of smoke across the open and fanned the raging flames to fury, set new fires.

The syndicate men milled helplessly in the clearing, coughing in the acrid fumes and pawing at their tear-filled eyes. A few ran toward the creek with pails and buckets —one carried a battered tin cup.

Potak ran to the ranch house to warn the sleeping owners. Yet even as he reached the broad veranda, the door came banging open and Bast and Brux came lurching out, cursing and clawing on their clothes. There was a black smudge across the face of the taciturn Brux who glared about him wildly.

"Some damn fool didn't watch where he threw his cigarette—"

A snarled curse from Bast cut Potak off. "Cigarette, hell! A quirley wouldn't start fires in three places at the same time, yuh knothead! This is Smith's work, damn his soul, an' I'll prove it 'fore I get through with him!"

Potak was about to speak again when a rider came pounding into the clearing, flung from the back of his heaving horse and came sprinting toward them. It was Dixon, and his harsh, hard-chiseled face was white.

"What you fools been up to?" he gasped out hoarsely.

"Aw, we been playin' with matches!" Bast snarled with a heavy sarcasm. "Where in hell you been?"

Three dark-garbed horsemen, entering the mouth of Grasshopper Draw, looked back across their shoulders. The night was still black, yet far off to the southwest, a point of light was flickering, red against the sky.

One of the shadowy riders chuckled. "I didn't think yuh had it in yuh, son. I reckon I was some mistook."

The three rode on again in silence, rode slowly now for there was lather on their horses' flanks. For a time the soft plop-plop of hoofs in sand was the only sound. Then the leader spoke:

"Shucks, Buck. When folks gets tuh proddin' me obstreperous-like, I always figger it's good policy tuh knock 'em down and kick out some of their teeth!"

CHAPTER XIII

The Dude Shows His Hand

Hardly had Old Sol's rays started climbing over the jagged eastern horizon than Smith was out of bed and on his way to the Big 3 headquarters. Most of the bandages with which he had been decorated, he had removed before starting.

He had told Willmoth where he was going and had intimated he was making the trip with the intention of making an effort to collect for his slaughtered sheep. It was, he thought, quite possible that the railroad would stand the damages, but he did not intend to overlook any bets.

Despite his recent defeat in town, the gunless outlander seemed in fine fettle this sunshiny morn. It was six miles from the Smithers place to the Big 3 outfit on Crawling Dog Crick and Smith tok his time getting there. He could find no sense in steaming his horse all up on the journey over, especially as he might wish to leave the enemy camp in somewhat of a hurry. In which case it would be worth something to have a horse that was fairly fresh.

Arriving at Big 3 headquarters, the Smiler glanced round with great surprise at the group of grim-faced men that stood about the clearing staring gloomily at the smouldering remains of what had once been a group of fine log buildings.

Among the gloomy watchers, Smith saw Brux, Dixon, and Bast. The latter was in a black rage and was palpably drunk. With sudden sharp sound of indrawn breath, the uninvited visitor noted that every man in the clearing was armed; some with rifles, all with holstered pistols.

Nevertheless, his customary drawl was just as taunting when he spoke:

"Howdy, gents. You, too, Bast. Been havin' quite a bonfire, looks like."

Threatening scowls creased the soot-smeared faces of the men nearest Smith, but he appeared not to notice.

Bast swung round with a ready oath. "You're sure got yore guts, comin' over here this mornin', Smith! By cripes, I got a notion——"

"Then be kind to it, fella. It's in a mighty strange place," the Smiler chuckled.

"Yeah? Yuh think so?" Bast walked over to where Smith sat his horse so nonchalantly and thrust his snarling features close, his odd-shaped head seeming more than ever like a toad on a lumpy rock.

"If you was half a man," he gritted, "yuh'd tote a gun, 'stead of ridin' round the country like a durn tenderfoot! An' if you was totin' a gun, I'd put yuh in a coffin, so dang quick yuh'd never know what struck yuh!"

"Moral—don't never pack hardware when yuh go to visit Bast," Smith drawled.

"Think you're funny, don't yuh. But the laugh will be on the other side of yore face when we get done with yuh!"

"There you go! Vindictiveness again," Smith heaved up a gusty sigh. "Why can't you jaspers imbibe a little Christian spirit? What have I done now to hurt your little pink feelin's?"

"Done! *Done!*" Bast cursed with a will, and meant it.

Virtuous bewilderment stamped Smith's open countenance as he listened in open-mouthed astonishment to the cattleman's sizzling oaths. "Whew!" he said, wiping his perspiring forehead with the back of a sleeve, "you'd ought to charge admission for a speech like that!"

Bast choked, his features purple with impotent anger. "Get out! Get out!" he spluttered. "Gun or no gun, next time I sight yuh I'm shootin' tuh kill!"

With doleful countenance and muttered words about "loving your neighbor" Smith turned his horse and prepared to depart. Jud Dixon, however, striding up, yelled for him to wait a minute.

"How'd you happen to ride over here this morning, Smith?"

"Why, Tranter an' Willmoth an' myself were down to Grasshopper Draw las' night lookin' at some strange white-faced cattle what was grazin' on S-Bar-S range. We poked around for quite a while, sort of estimatin' how many head we was goin' to have to charge you fellas for. All of a sudden we seen a red flare in the sky over this way. So this mornin' I rode over tuh see what you fellas been up to. Looks like Judgment Day round here this mornin'."

"Feeling pretty gay with yourself, ain't yuh?" a scowl twisted Dixon's harsh face. "I hope you can prove them words, Mister—you an' your hired rustlers," he said portentously, and walked away.

Jogging slowly homeward, Dixon's remark gave Smith some food for thought.

By noon, the same day, the Big Three had moved bag and baggage into an old, unused line camp a short half mile from the entrance to Grasshopper Draw. If they felt their new headquarters was a come-down from the luxury of their old, they consoled themselves with the reflection come necessary, they felt, to be where they could keep an eye on their cattle, the majority of which were now feeding contentedly on Smith's grass.

The line camp shelter was a long, low shack surmounting a slight rise in plain sight of the trail that led through the draw to Smith's ranch. The shack was partially screened on the side facing the draw by a scrubby stand of pinions. Behind the shack stretched away into the distance the sandstone crags and spires and shale and lava of the Devil's Boot. Desolate, grim, forbidding.

The syndicate punchers were promptly put to work by Brux at felling some of the larger trees. From these, Brux aimed to build a bunkhouse in due time. A corral was unnecessary, since the old one was easily put in repair.

About two hours after the Big Three's shift in quarters, Dixon—standing in the doorway—made out through the pinons the figure of an approaching horseman jogging toward the shack from the direction of the draw.

He called Bast. The thick-set man of action took one look and swore. "What's that durn scissor bill want?"

"He's probably got some information for us." Dixon's tone was cold. "See that you keep a civil tongue in your head while he's here. I'll do the talkin'."

Monahan rode through the trees and dismounted before the door. Dixon led the way inside, the dude and Bast entering after him. All three took chairs.

"Heard you gents had a fire last night," Monahan's hard eyes held a sardonic twinkle. "Did you get burnt out?"

Bast glowered and clenched his fists. Dixon said:

"Somebody dumped some coal oil on three of our buildin's and threw some matches in it; sparks an' the wind did the rest. What do you know about it?"

Monahan's lips curled back in a grin that revealed his flashing teeth; he winked knowingly at Bast. "Smith an' them hired hands of his wasn't at the ranch the biggest part of last night." He looked at Dixon's expressionless face. "That mean anything?"

"It might," Bast growled, "if you'd swear yuh trailed

'em over to our headquarters an' saw 'em set the place afire!"

"What would it be worth to you birds to have me perjure myself that way?" Monahan asked after a moment.

"It would depend," said Dixon suavely, "on how useful your perjury turned out."

"I don't guess I'd care to do any swearin' in that case," Monahan scratched his long neck as he stared from one to the other of the cattlemen.

Dixon watched him thoughtfully. What the dude had said about Smith and his men being away a good portion of the previous night, checked with what Smith himself had said. Nevertheless, Dixon thought that if things broke right and if he was able to muzzle Bast long enough, he'd have Smith just where he wanted him. "Any more information on tap this mornin'? If not, we got work to do an' will have to ask yuh to step over some other time when we ain't so busy."

"Well, I'll be sayin' so long, then." Monahan put on the battered Stetson he had borrowed from Smith's bunkhouse to replace his lost derby and started for the door, giving Bast a wink as he did so. Bast followed him out. When they reached a point beyond earshot of the shack, the dude said:

"I got some more information, Mister Bast, but I ain't givin' it out for nothin'. I don't aim to do no more stoolpigeonin' for a short sport like that dang Dixon, either. If I'm gonna collect information for you birds, I expect to get paid for it."

"Well, that's all right," the heavy-set cattleman's blackstubbled face expanded in a genial grin. "Dixon *is* a mite tight, for a fact. Spill your information an' if I think I can use it I'll pay yuh what it's worth to me."

"It's about that dame that's keepin' house for Smith."

"The Dolores filly, eh?" Bast's pale piggish eyes showed interest. "I'm listenin'."

"After Smith an' them tough hands of his pulled out last night, I went up to the house," Monahan said. "I didn't have no trouble gettin' in. The dame had her door barred, but I got it open an' got into her room without wakin' her up. I was aiming to take a look at that gold locket she wears, but jest as I reached for it she kind of sighed an' turned over."

"Humph! What did yuh figger was in the locket?"

"Pictures, of course—"

"Well, I ain't buyin' any pictures today," Bast growled.

"Hold on," Monahan sneered as the cattleman started to turn away. "I ain't tryin' to sell you any pictures. Don't be a bigger chump than nature made you! If I'm right, the pictures in that locket'll interest you about as much as anything ever could. You want to snag Smith, don't you?"

"Yeah. I'm gonna, too. What's the gal's locket got to do with Smith?"

"Plenty," said Monahan.

Smiling Smith, when he reached the S-Bar-S, stripped the gear from Flea-Bite and turned him into the corral after giving him some oats. Then he strode toward the veranda where Tranter sat with his feet on the rail and his battered pipe between his lips.

"Where's Willmoth?" Smith asked. "I see his horse has gone. Hasn't quit us, has he?"

"Nope; the Yeller-Shoes dude went for a ride an' Willmoth opined it might be a right good idee tuh trail along behind him. He thinks Monahan's up tuh somethin's slimy. As soon's the dude got outa sight, Willmoth got his nag an' started after him. Did we do a good job las' night?"

Smith chuckled. "The Big 3 are gonna move, I reckon. Some nasty gent set their home ranch on fire last night an' it burned plumb to the ground, Buck. I felt awful sorry for 'em, but they didn't seem tuh care for my brand of sympathy. How's Dolo?"

"She's gettin' dinner, I reckon. Wonder where the Big 3 will move to? Gosh, I'd like to of seen their faces this mornin'." Unscrewing the stem from his pipe, Tranter blew through it vigorously and polished it on his frazzled corduroy trousers. "Prancin' prairie dogs! I bet them gents was some mad at losin' that there purty ranch house an' out-buildin's!"

"They didn't seem real pleased about it. Bast did a lot of splutterin', but Dixon looked kinda mean. He said he hoped we could prove where we was last night. He's a deep one, that Dixon jasper. What do yuh think, Buck, about dammin' up Crawlin' Dog Crick an' cuttin' off the Big 3 water supply?"

"Cripes!" Tranter stared. "I don't think much of the idea, if you're askin' me real serious. That would be the last straw fer them syndicate polecats. They'd come over here with their hired guns an' blood in their eye. No, I don't reckon we'd better figger on doin' nothin' that drastic just yet. It wouldn't get us anything, no way. All the syndicate cattle is in our valley right now. You better spend your time figgerin' how to get 'em back where they belong before they chew our range to the roots!"

Smith nodded, looked out across the valley in the direction of Grasshopper Draw. "Looks like Willmoth ridin' this way."

Tranter looked. "Yeah, that's Trigger. I wonder where he left the dude?"

"An' I'm wonderin'," Smith said grimly, "just what Dixon meant by that remark of his. I'd give somethin' to look into his mind for about two minutes. I got a notion that hombre is cookin' up somethin' that'll make us sick."

Tranter scowled. "Dixon's a real cold-deck artist, all right. Like I said before, this business will come tuh powdersmoke, yet. Don't never doubt it, Smiler. You take the word of a man what knows: the Big 3 is goin' to get this spread or bust a gut tryin'."

When Trigger Willmoth reached the ranch he rode directly to the veranda before dismounting. As he swung from the saddle there was a mean look in his eyes. He threw a leg over the railing and lounged there.

"Big Three have moved their movables an' taken a lease on that line camp t'other side of Grasshopper Draw," he said with a cold grin, and drew the "makings" from his pocket. "Them fellas mean business, Smiler."

Smith regarded him through narrowed eyes.

"Where'd yuh leave the dude?" Tranter asked.

"I left him visitin' with Bast an' Dixon."

"I always knowed yuh couldn't trust a man what would wear yeller shoes," Tranter grunted, eyeing Smith reproachfully. "Didn't I tell yuh dudes was more bother than they was worth?"

But the Smiler wasn't listening. "Any syndicate men in Smithers Valley?"

"Uh-uh," Willmoth shook his head. "They're all busy choppin' trees over there by their new headquarters." His puckered gray eyes studied the cigarette he was rolling with expert fingers. "I watched the place for awhile through the binoculars. After a while the dude come out of the shack with Bast. They stopped by the pinons for a spell. The dude's jaw was waggin' real earnest. He'll bear a bit o' watchin'."

"Monahan can't prove where we was last night," Smith said after several minutes had passed in silence.

"Naw," Tranter growled, "but he won't have much trouble provin' we wasn't home!"

"His word against ours—an' there's three of us to one of him," Smith pointed out.

"Jest the same," said Tranter, "if yuh'll take a little *ad*vice from a fella that's been around, yuh'll get rid of that dude as soon as he comes back. Hand him his walkin' papers an' put him on a nag!"

CHAPTER XIV

A POTENT STINGER

ABOUT an hour after Willmoth's return, Smith and Tranter, still lounging on the cool veranda, beheld a whirl of dust moving leisurely up the valley trail.

"A hell-bent soul rides yonder," Tranter grunted after watching it several moments. "That's Bast, all by his lonesome, an' comin' tuh pay us a call."

Smith nodded. "You got good eyes, Buck—reg'lar buzzard eyes."

"Shucks," the shaggy foreman scoffed, "it ain't no trouble to pick out a gent's identity at that measly distance. A kid c'ld do as good! Why, when I was a little shaver, no more'n knee-high to a prairiedog's neck, my folks used to live up in the Ozark Mountings. We had us a shack on Blackberry Ridge, twenty-five miles from the ol' dead tree on Shoestring Hill. Wal, I used to set around on our doorstep of a sunny day an' watch woodpeckers drill holes in the bark o' that tree. I had pretty fair eyesight, them days."

"I'll say," Smith chuckled. "Tell me another."

"You don't think," Tranter's look held reproach, "I been lyin', do yuh?"

"Wonder what Willmoth is settin' on the bunkhouse steps with that rifle for?"

"Probably spotted Bast a-comin' same as I did. Willmoth's like me, he's a gent as believes in bein' prepared. Reckon our unwelcome visitor'll be here in haff an hour, or so. Ho-hum," Tranter pulled his battered pipe from the hip pocket of his corduroy trousers, loaded it with tobacco which he whittled from a plug. "The trouble I've seen is enough tuh make a body callous. I reckon I'll be seein' a heap more before this week is out. The Big 3 has used a deal more patience with yuh now, Smiler, than I ever figgered 'em capable of doing."

"You better go round to the kitchen an' talk with Dolo while Bast's payin' his visit," Smith said abruptly. "I don't want her comin' out here while that polecat's around."

"Hmm," Tranter said, and gave the Smiler a curious look. "Hmm," and getting to his feet, he sauntered off, smoking his evil-smelling pipe.

Big Al Bast, when he arrived at the S-Bar-S, did not dismount. He sat his hammer-headed roan before the veranda railing and eyed Smith with a hostile stare.

"What the heck's eatin' *you?*" Smith greeted.

Darts of flame flecked the piggish eyes of Bast. A cruel, mirthless smile played across his fat, black-stubbled face. "I come tuh talk about that fire we had at the Big 3 last night," he growled. "You durn near put one over on us that time—but not quite. How much cash you figgerin' to pay us for that little joke?"

Smith laughed. "If you're tryin tuh insinuate I had anything tuh do with your bonfire, you're crazy as a bed bug. I ain't aimin' tuh pay you one lousy cent."

"No?" Bast grinned malevolently. "Wal, think again, young fella. You'll pay, all right, or go tuh jail. Yuh can take your choice. We got a eye-witness what saw you ride outa here las' night an' trailed yuh and yore hired rustlers over to our place. He saw you jaspers take them cans of oil outa our storage shed, spill oil on three of our buildin's an' set 'em afire Now—do yuh pay up or don't yuh?"

Smith struggled to realize what had happened, and suddenly it opened up before him—the dude dick from El Paso had been working overtime and blabbed his discoveries to the Big Three. Just as Tranter and Willmoth had warned him Monahan would. It looked like Bast had him this time.

Bast, watching him like a hawk eyeing a chicken, saw cold humor glinting in Smith's frosty eyes. The thick-set rancher was puzzled. Had Smith found a loophole somewhere——an alibi that would discount the dude's testimony? Not that he intended buying such a false statement from Monahan; but he had hoped to scare Smith into a damaging admission. Judging by the look in Smith's eyes, he was going to be disappointed.

He was.

"Interestin' if true," said the Smiler, with a hard laugh.

"It's true, all right! You'll find it don't pay tuh buck the Big Three, Mister!"

"Even if yuh could prove I set your place afire, which yuh can't," Smith grinned, "you still wouldn't have any kick after derailin' three cars of my sheep at Big Bend trestle!"

"The skunk that says we done that is a slat-bellied liar!" Bast snarled.

"The jasper that told yuh he saw us settin' fire to your buildin's ain't no purveyor of Gospel."

"We'll skip that for the moment," Bast said. His eyes narrowed ominously as he thrust his toad-like head forward on his massive shoulders. "But here's somethin' you ain't a-goin' to side-step, Mister. Get rid of that damn gun-slingin' rustler, Tranter, inside the next twenty-four hours or I'll have the sheriff out here with a warrant for you an' him both!"

Bast's pale venomous glance locked with the cold blue glaze of Smith. For a space of time in which a leisurely man might count to ten, there was silence. Then a cold grin parted Smith's hard lips.

"Go tuh the devil," he drawled.

The cattleman swayed forward in his saddle and his hand swept down to leather. Murder flamed in his slitted eyes.

"That's right," Smith taunted him recklessly. "Pull that smoke-pole if you're huntin' a quick grave."

Bast shot a hasty look over his shoulder and saw Willmoth on the bunkhouse steps with a rifle in his hands.

Without another word he turned his horse and, with a

savage jab of the spurs, went pounding off.

When Bast reached the new headquarters of the Big Three, Jud Dixon was just swinging from the back of a lathered horse.

"I wanta see you in the house," he said, "soon's you get the gear stripped off that roan."

When Bast entered their new quarters a short time later, Dixon swung round and stopped his nervous pacing. "Where have you been?" he demanded curtly.

The thick-set man regarded the speaker in some surprise. "What's got you on the prod?" he countered.

"There's hell poppin' in Bucksnort. Some lousy son put a bullet through Si Jones last night an' cleaned out his private safe!"

Bast's jaw sagged open and hung that way.

"The whole durn town's stirred up. If they ever get their hands on the guy that did it—"

Bast suddenly grinned. "Cripes! What's wrong with hangin' it onto Smith?"

"That's an idea I been thinkin' about," Dixon admitted softly. "His hat was found on the floor near the safe. Now, suppose you tell me where you been since dinner? It looked to me like you was comin' back from the Smithers place."

"I was," Bast chuckled. "Gosh, Jud, but I sure read the riot act tuh Smith! I sure got him green with fright! I told him we had a eye-witness what saw him an' them hired gun-slingers of his set fire to our place last night. Cripes, yuh oughta seen him takin' water! I told him right in front of that pucker-eyed Willmoth jasper that he could either get rid of Tranter inside of twenty-four hours or I'd have the sheriff out there with a warrant for 'em both! I— What's the matter, Jud?"

Dixon's hard-chiseled face was gray.

"Yuh got a belly-ache, or somethin'?"

Dixon's bright-button glance was a blaze of fury.

"Yeah, I got a belly-ache—and how! Al Bast, you're a plain dang fool!"

"Huh? What the—"

"Shut up! I'm doin' the talkin' now!" Dixon's tone still was soft, but venom oozed from it as he shoved the words out, one by one, between his teeth. "Here we had Smith just where we wanted him for once; half the town knows he's been tryin' to get a loan from the bank an' there was his Stetson layin' on the floor by Si's gutted safe an' only a coupla feet from Si's blood-smeared corpse. An' you had tuh go over to the S-Bar-S an' tell them fellas yuh had a witness that could swear he saw 'em at *our place* last night settin' a *fire!* You got real brains in your bullet head! G'wan! git outa here 'fore I forget you're my pardner an' do yuh a hurt!"

"But—but how was I tuh know Si Jones got himself killed last night?" Bast protested. "An' that Smith's Stetson was found by his safe?"

"What I'd admire to learn," said Dixon flatly, "is how you know enough to go in when it rains!"

Tranter and his boss were sitting on the shady veranda, smoking while they waited for supper, when Monahan returned. Tranter got up to take care of the dude's horse.

"Sit down," Smith's tone was gruff. "The dude ain't stoppin' long—not long enough to put that hawss up."

As Monahan reined in before the house and climbed out of the saddle, Smith strode forward to meet him, and his face was cold and grim.

"Been visitin' our neighbors?"

Monahan looked his host over insolently. "Since you ask, buddy, I don't mind admittin' I have," he replied, coolly.

"Have a good time talkin' with Bast?"

The dude's eyes flickered strangely. "Is it a custom out here to put shadows on a guest every time he leaves the house?"

"Depends some on the guest, I reckon," Smith drawled. "There's a snake or two on this range that'll bear watchin' all the time."

"Was that crack aimed at me."

"If the boot fits, pardner, pull it on." There was no threat, no animosity in the Smiler's tone; a soft suggestion soberly voiced. But the dude's green eyes grew wary.

"Kind of hostile tonight, ain't yuh, Smithy? Somebody step on your pet corn?"

"I got no use for a gent that'll eat a man's salt an' sell him out behind his back. Ain't it the truth that you went over to the Big 3 line-camp the other side of Grasshopper Draw on purpose to tell that bunch of range-hawgs that me an' the boys was away last night?"

Monahan's lips curled slightly. "What if it is? No law to the contrary, is there?"

"In New Mexico, Mister, we have a few laws what ain't on on the statute books. You better get back on that hawss an start makin' tracks. You're through here. Your kind ain't wanted on the S-Bar-S. . . . We prefer our side-winders with buttons on 'em!"

"Buttons—"

"Yeah. We like tuh hear 'em rattle 'fore they strike."

Monahan saw something in Smith's eyes he did not like. But he was no weak-kneed mealy-mouth, and he had done his share of brow-beating as a detective in El Paso. He had no notion of quiting cold just because this Smith was getting a little salty.

"I paid for a month's vacation here, buddy, an' I still got another week to go. Climb down off your high horse an' act like a gentleman, even if you ain't nothin' but the hind end of a cow's—"

"As I was sayin'," Smith cut in, "you better get on that hawss an' start makin' tracks. If yuh rile me into losin' my temper I sh'n't be responsible for what happens. You've paid for a week yuh ain't gettin'—but you're gettin' a durn fine hawss yuh ain't paid for. If there's any loss to this deal you ain't the loser."

"Hard guy, ain't you?" Monahan sneered. "When I get through with you an' that half-breed dame——"

He broke off as Smith started toward him, his eyes like chips of ice.

"Another yip outa you, coyote, an' I'll——" Smith turned away with a disgusted snort. The Monahan dick from Texas was pounding down the trail in a rising cloud of dust.

Tranter took the pipe from his mouth, looked at his boss and shook his head.

"Yuh made a mistake," he growled, "when yuh let that scorpion git away. Yuh should of put yore lead down hard an' squashed him, Smiler. You've left his stinger potent an' he shore won't rest till he proves it!"

CHAPTER XV

BLOOD ON THE MOON

"SHUCKS," said Smith, unruffled by his foreman's gloomy prophecy. "You're gettin' mighty nigh vindictive as that Bast fella. Y'ought to be ashamed of yourself, talkin' that way. It don't conform good to the policy of this here rancho. The S-Bar-S, Mister Tranter, is a peaceful outfit —even if its owner does act like a—a—a—What did he call me?"

Tranter chuckled: "A cow's hind end!"

"Well, I'd rather be that than the kind of jasper he is! Such colossal gall—eatin' our victuals an' sellin' us down the crik!"

"I warned yuh," grunted Tranter, "that dudes was poison. But yuh would have 'em. Yuh better pray no more of 'em answers that fool ad of yorn. That fella's goin' to make you more trouble 'fore he gets planted or run out of the country."

"Shucks," Smith said, and changed the subject. "Reckon I'll go tuh town first thing in the mornin' an—"

"Seems like goin' tuh town is gettin' tuh be a reg'lar habit with you," Tranter interrupted. "That's another of them things I warned yuh about. You'll ride tuh town once too often one of these days an' there'll a spurt o' flame, a puff o' smoke, an' a coffin on the S-Bar-S!"

"You sure believe in tellin' it creepy, fella."

"I don't tell it no more creepy than what Bast an' his buddies would like tuh have it," Tranter muttered. "There's times, Smiler, when you act plain foolish. I guess it must be the fault of them Christian sentiments you're allus talkin' about."

Smith grinned. "Tuh, tut, ol'-timer, an' again tut. Yuh ought to sign up with some flourishin' undertaker—you're gettin' so you hand crepe real well. Gettin back to what I was sayin' when yuh interrupted, I'm figgerin' to go in to Bucksnort in the mornin' an' in-stitoot proceedin's against the Big 3 for slander. They've accused us of settin' that fire they had last night an' claim they got a eye-witness to prove it.

"Eye-witnesses, Tranter, is dang unreliable things to bank on—specially, the one they got. Which is Monahan. Now when they put that dude on the stand I'll discredit his testimony in two shakes of a steer's horn! I'll tell the Court how we had a row here this afternoon an' I sent the dude a-packin'. Naturally he's feelin' a mite peeved. A fella in his state o' mind wouldn't think nothin' at all of committin' perjury. I'll also point out he used to be a city dick. From then on, any jury in the country'll dump the case right in our lap!"

Tranter looked at his boss with a glance in which admiration seemed well-blended with natural pessimism. "Wal," he said. "I hope you're right."

The next morning dawned as most mornings dawn in New Mexico—fair and warmer.

A pale blue sky stretched above the desert country like a benediction and the sun, as it climbed above the horizon, gilded the sandstone spires in the distant Devil's Boot with its golden rays that picked out here and there lavender patches of shadow and illumined the vermilion streaks in the strata.

It was such a morning as the Great Boss fashions for lovers, so it was not strange that Smiling Smith should ask Dolores to ride townward with him when the breakfast things were cleared away.

"Thought mebbe yuh might be wantin' a new dress or two," he stammered, blushing.

So it was that an hour later Smith and his ragged housekeeper set out from the S-Bar-S a-horseback. The pungent tang of sage was in the air, and there was a touch of warming color in the girl's golden cheeks and a dancing imp of laughter in her long-lashed dusky eyes.

"That Tranter," the girl spoke after riding some while in silence, "he knows that Bast weel send the sheriff for him. We heard your honor tell him that you would not do as he weeshed," her eyes were bright with approval.

"Shucks," Smith said, and changed the subject. "Reckon I'll have to get me some more wire. Seems like it might be a good idea to fence them syndicate cattle in, so's to be sure they stay on our range. That way I can charge the Big 3 a stiff grazin' fee. If they won't pay it I'll have some reason for hangin' onto their beef."

But Dolores was not interested in syndicates, barbwire, grazing fees or cattle, so she changed the conversation and they spoke of other things more interesting to a young girl deep in love.

About half an hour after they had left Grasshopper Draw to the rear, Smith chanced to glance behind him and spied two horsemen. Bast and Potak, he thought, and wondered if any particular reason was taking them to town.

Smith and Dolores reached Bucksnort shortly before

noon. The town was abuzz with some exciting happening, Smith perceived no sooner than they reached it. There was an air, an atmosphere of tensity that rasped upon the nerves.

Smith headed their horses for the general store and they swung from the saddles before the long pole hitch-rail. Hardly had the Smiler's booted feet slapped earth than a burly man with ferocious-looking walrus mustache came down the steps and stepped up to him.

"Howdy, Sheriff," Smith grinned. "Long time no see you."

"Yeah, must be almost a couple days since we last met," Hellman answered drily. Much of his former cordiality appeared to have left him, Smith thought. "Where was you the night before last, young fella?"

Smith grinned. "There's more jaspers interested in where I was the night 'fore last than yuh could shake a stick at. Me an' Tranter an' Willmoth—which same is my punchers—was down lookin' over some syndicate cattle what had been shoved on our range by way of Grasshopper Draw. Some of them ornery Big 3 jaspers tore down our fences an'—"

"You got proof of that, hev yuh? Proof yuh wasn't in town that night?"

"Well, gosh a'mighty! What happened in town, anyways?"

"Si Jones was killed an' the jasper what done it gutted the safe in his private office!" the Sheriff said, and there was a glitter in his eyes. "Yuh want to change that statement of yours now?"

"Nope," Smith said. "I'm sure some surprised to hear that Jones was killed, though I guess, judgin' by the way you're lookin' at me, he was murdered. Was he?"

"He was."

Smith was a great deal more surprised than he was letting on. Why anyone should have wanted to snuff Si Jones was, in Smith's opinion, a pretty puzzle. It did not seem worth the risk entailed. He looked at Dolores and grinned. "You better go on in the store an' be pickin' out whatever things yuh'd like tuh have," he said. "I'll be in after I get through talkin' with Dan here."

When Dolores had gone inside the general store, Smith asked:

"Who do yuh reckon done it?"

Sheriff Hellman eyed him speculatively. "There's a number of gents that think you did, Smith. I ain't sayin' what I believe. I will say this much, though: about every-one in town knows you been tryin' tuh borry money from the bank; quite a number of folks know that you an' Jones didn't get along; *I* know that your J. B. hat was found within two feet of Jones' body."

Smith was swift to get the significance of the lawman's last remark. It looked like things dovetailed a bit too nicely to be the work of chance. He could see a careful hand in this business—a hand that was trying to frame him for the banker's murder.

"My hat was found beside the body, eh?" Smith's gaze became vacuous, thoughtful. "Seems like somebody's got it in for me. You recollect when I rode outa town day 'fore yesterday I wasn't wearin' any hat. I lost the old one I was wearin' that day durin' the fracas in the Tall Bottle. . . . I wonder just what time Jones was killed?"

"The coroner thinks it was around twelve-thirty."

"Where did yuh say you found him?"

"I didn't say," Hellman's tone was dry. "It happens that the cashier of the bank found him the followin' morn-ing when the bank opened for business. Jones was layin' in his private office on the floor near his desk. Your hat was close by and the door of Si's private safe was open an' most of the contents strewn around the office like whoever killed Jones was lookin' for somethin'."

"Hmm. It strikes me that it might be interestin' tuh know what Si was doin' in the bank after office hours— especially at that time o' night," Smith said, and looked

Hellman in the eye. "Kinda odd, don't you reckon?"

"Whoever killed him mighta forced him to go to the bank—"

"On the other hand," Smith pointed out, "he might have gone there on his own hook to meet some gent who didn't care to have his business known by the whole town. Then, there's other reasons why he might have gone to the bank in the middle of the night."

"Such as—?"

Smith grinned. "Don't ask me, Sheriff. I ain't no mind-reader." But, to himself, Smith was thinking the banker might have gone there to get some papers or to gather up his personal assets in preparation to leaving the country. Jones, to Smith's knowledge, had changed climates once; he might have been about to repeat the process.

"Who's the best lawyer in town, Sheriff?" he asked abruptly.

The lawman's shaggy eyebrows rose. He eyed Smith intently. "There's only two," he said, at last. "Neither of 'em's anything tuh brag on. The syndicate patronizes Timothy Klain—his office is upstairs in the bank buildin'. The other fella is Tom Sleen; his sign's hung out above the Santa Fe Restaurant."

"Well, thanks for the information, Sheriff. Yuh want me to come in for the inquest on Jones?"

"The inquest on Jones has been held already. Coroner Beekman is a fast-worker," Hellman said. "His jury returned an opinion of 'Killed by person or persons unknown,' with a strong recommendation to investigate your whereabouts at time of death."

"Shucks," Smith grinned despite the seriousness of the situation. "I never hide my light under no bushel—my actions is always open to investigation. If you can prove I wasn't where I said I was the night before last, you go right ahead an' do so."

As Smiling Smith strode down the street in the direction of the Santa Fe Restaurant, leaving the sheriff staring after him thoughtfully, he was in high good humor with himself. This business of the murdered banker and Smith's hat being found beside his body showed nasty intentions toward the boss of the S-Bar-S on the part of some underhanded jasper. It was on a par with the horse trick played on him by Potak.

But Bast had unintentionally saved his bacon. Smith chuckled when he thought of the weapon Big Al had blunderingly placed in his hands.

Reaching the restaurant, Smith pulled open a door on the side of the frame building and, after mounting a long flight of dark and narrow stairs, knocked on a door whose upper panel was of frosted glass. A nasal voice bade him enter.

A lean, sallow-faced man sat picking his teeth behind a battered desk. He looked Smith over curiously, but did not speak.

"Are you Mister Tom Sleen, the lawyer?"

The sallow-faced man nodded indifferently and continued picking his teeth.

"Business pretty good these days?" Smith asked, irritated by Sleen's attitude.

"Oh, so-so. Business ain't never anything to get het up over in a cattle town," the lawyer grunted, momentarily suspending operations with his toothpick. "Law an' the cow business ain't never done no hugging an' kissing that I've heard tell of."

Smith chuckled. "Well, don't look so down in the mouth. I've got some business for you. If yuh put it over I'll see that yuh get plenty of business in the future. I want you to start slander proceedin's against the Big 3 syndicate—"

"Nope," the lawyer grimaced. "I can't help you. You and I can't do no business that would be unfavorable to the interests of the Big 3. I accepted a retainer from Jud Dixon yesterday mornin'. Sorry, but I'll have to bid you good-day, now. I'm kinda busy this forenoon."

When Smith emerged from the lawyer's office into the bright sunlight of the street, there was a thoughtful frown on his lean, hard-bitten face. Plainly, he thought, Jud Dixon was the brains of the syndicate. Equally plain to Smith was the fact that Dixon was a man who looked ahead, figuring to the best of his ability—which seemed pretty good—just what an opponent might be most apt to do next and checkmating the move in advance.

Well, there seemed nothing to do but make a stab at interesting the other lawyer, the man usually patronized by the Big Three. With this thought in mind, Smith started for the bank building, deciding to stop in at the Tall Bottle on the way and wet his whistle.

There were no customers in the Tall Bottle saloon this morning but Al Bast and two of the syndicate gun-toters—Jed Harmon, and his side-kick "Lefty" Flynn. Harmon was short, dark and swarthy. Flynn was rangy, red-headed, and had a cast in his right eye.

Though Potak had ridden in with Bast this morning, he was not in the saloon at the moment.

Bast signalled the bartender, who was fat like most of his kind, and ordered a round of drinks for himself and his two men. Harmon and Flynn showed signs of interest at the possibility of a free drink.

"Mebbe that hombre you're waitin' for won't come in this mornin'," the barman ventured, setting glasses and a bottle before the customers.

"Shucks, he's been comin' to town every morning, pretty near, since he squatted on our range," Bast sneered. "Anyhow, he came to town this mornin'. Me an' Potak rode in behind him an' that Dolores filly he keeps out at his place."

"No; what I meant was, how do you know this Smith fella will be comin' in here?" the man behind the "mahogany" explained. "After that ruction you fellas had here a coupla days ago, I should think he'd be careful to steer clear of this place."

"A salty jasper like Smith wouldn't let a little thing like that keep him away if he wanted a drink," Bast said, with rare insight. "He'll stop in here sometime today, an' when he does I'm aimin' to be right on tap."

"What are yuh figgerin' tuh pay us for this business, Al?" asked Flynn. "We don't wanta go up ag'in no dang hurricane like that jasper for no forty a month an' found."

"Nobody's askin' yuh to." Bast looked his gunhands over appraisingly. He did not care to throw his hard-earned money away needlessly; still, it would be worth considerable to be able to look Dixon in the eye and say: "I may have pulled a boner on that fire deal, Jud, but I've squared it up for yuh, now. We salted Smith away in town this mornin' an' there wasn't any witnesses around tuh say he didn't have a break."

So thinking, Bast grinned at his men and said softly:

"It'll be worth a hundred an' fifty apiece to you gents tuh put Smith in a pine box. Does that sound?"

Flynn chuckled. "That sounds," he admitted, and his partner nodded his satisfaction.

Finishing their drinks the three men turned around and faced the swinging doors, leaning against the bar, their elbows resting on its edge.

As time passed and no untoward event marred the silence of the forenoon, Bast began to get uneasy. "What the heck's keepin' the fool?" he growled. "Ed," he called to the barkeep, "go up to the front there by the window an' see if you can see Smith outside any place."

"Don't see him," the man said, after a careful glance about the sunsplashed street. "His nag an' another one with his brand on it is standing in front of the general store. Guess probably he's inside gettin' provisions. Potak is comin' down the street. Looks like he's aimin' to go in the store, too."

Bast grinned to himself. He knew what Potak was going into the general store for; he had put the foreman up to it himself. He wished he could be down there, watching.

Suddenly the man staring out the window stiffened. "He's comin' now, gents," he muttered. "He just came out of Sleen's office an' he's comin' up the street headin' right for here straight as a riflebarrel."

Bast grinned malevolently. "Spread out a mite, fellas," he said softly. "Get someplace where yuh won't be slingin' your lead toward each other when the shootin' starts."

Lefty Flynn crossed to the far side of the room, pausing beside the piano with his left hand curled about the butt of his gun. Jed Harmon bow-legged his way to one of the deserted card tables halfway down the room, and turning it over so that one edge of its top rested on the flor, got behind it and drew his gun. Bast stayed where he was by the bar. "Get away from the window, Fat," he bade the barman.

"He's comin' towards the steps, now," said the man as he retreated.

"All right, boys," Bast growled softly and, drawing his own weapon, settled into a crouch with it leveled at the swinging doors. His gun-slingers, too, were crouching, heads thrust forward between their hunched shoulders, slitted eyes intent upon the entrance, six-guns held in ready grasp.

In the sudden silence, the ticking of the clock above the bar was like the banging of a monstrous gong.

"Don't do nothin' till he's pushed them slatted doors apart an' stands framed in th' openin'," Bast growled final instructions. "Then give him everything yuh got. Fire swift—an' shoot tuh kill!"

Back at the bunkhouse on the Smithers place, Buck Tranter put away his battered pipe and got up off his bunk. It was five minutes past twelve by his silver watch. "Cripes," he muttered, looking at Willmoth, a dark frown between his eyes. "This pistol-hoppin' foreman's job I got here at the S-Bar-S is enough tuh drive a ordinary jasper to drink an' smokin' locoweed. Peacefullest durn job I ever held down. That Big 3 crowd's a snare an' a delusion! They got a reputation fer bein' tough an' prancin' prairie chickens—a child of three could scare 'em with his shadder!"

"They're tough enough, I reckon," Willmoth bit off a generous chew of Tranter's plug of tobacco. Passing the diminished piece back to its owner, he masticated thoughtfully, deep lines of concentration between his puckered gray eyes.

"Yuh see," he announced presently, "Smith's sort of got the Injun sign on them fellas, Buck. They don't know how tuh take him, bein' as he don't tote no pistol. The Big 3 is used to dealin' with sixgun yankers an' rifle experts. They ain't had no experience with a two-fisted gent like the Smiler.

"But they'll learn. If they can't get rid of him by schemin' an tryin' tur frame him into a jam with the authorities, they'll shuck their hawglegs an' come a-smokin'. There's gonna be some gore spilled on this range before this thing gets settled; I can tell it by the shine of the moon."

Tranter snorted. "Stick around the ranch this afternoon, Trigger. Speakin' of the shine of the moon reminds me that I ain't had a drink for a heck of a while. I'm goin' tuh town. This durn alkali water has got my pipes all rusty."

"You better stay away from town. Yuh heard what Bast told the boss yesterday about swearin' out a warrant for yuh, didn't yuh? Well, he's takin' a chance keepin' yuh on—"

"Which is reason number two why I'm a-headin' fer town," Tranter growled, running a gnarled hand through his shaggy mane. "D'yuh think I aim tuh set here an' let that skunk swear out a warrant for the boss jest because he's too big-hearted tuh send me walkin' down the road? Wal, not so's yuh could notice it. I aim tuh fork a bronc tuh town an' hunt me up that sheriff. If there's any dang warrant swore out again' me, I reckon my ol' Betsy here can argue Dan Hellman into tearin' it up," and he slapped the weapon in the tied-down holster on his leg.

"Let's cut for it," Willmoth suggested. "I'd sorta like to go tuh town myself." Tranter wasn't fooling *him* any. Willmoth knew the foreman was worried about Smiling Smith. And, if the truth be told, Willmoth was doing a little worrying himself. The Big 3 had been behaving just a trifle too nicely for his peace of mind. Something was due to break, he told himself. There was violence in the very air.

Tranter eyed the sinewy, hawk-nosed man suspiciously, but feeling that he knew a thing or two about manipulating cards that Willmoth had never learned, he finally agreed and produced a dog-eared deck.

CHAPTER XVI

DOUBLE TROUBLE

As Smiling Smith came opposite the general store, next door to the Tall Bottle and on the same side of the street, he saw Dan Hellman coming out and waved an airy hand. The sheriff waved back and Smith waited. Probably the lawman had been inside to question Dolo, he thought. If so he had not learned a great deal, judging by his expression.

"I understand," said Hellman, joining him, "you got a dude stayin' out at your place. Is that so?"

"It ain't now," Smith grinned. "Him an' me passed a few words yesterday afternoon an' I told him to clear out. He didn't like it very much; acted sort of peeved. Said I was hooking him out of a week's board. But he didn't lose nothin'. I gave 'im the hawss he rode away on."

"What did yuh quarrel about, you an' this dude?" Hellman asked, failing into step beside the young rancher who was still moving toward the saloon.

"It's a sort of personal matter, Sheriff. I'd rather not discuss it."

Starting to mount the wooden steps leading onto the veranda of the Tall Bottle, Smith abruptly grabbed the lawman's arm. The veranda floor was on a level with Smith's keen eyes and he had perceived, beneath the swinging doors, the booted feet of a crouching man. He knew the fellow was crouching by the position of the feet. That one look was enough for Smith.

"Let's go round to the rear door," he muttered in the sheriff's ear.

Hellman looked at him in some surprise, but offered no objections. They passed an alley to the rear entrance, which they found unlocked. Smith opened the door softly and he and Hellman stepped inside. They passed down a narrow hallway and the next moment found themselves inside the resort's main room. Three men were crouched there in attitudes of waiting. Each man had a ready weapon in his hand; each man's eyes fixed intently on the swinging doors of the front entrance.

Smith looked at Hellman and found him scowling. Smiler grinned; Hellman might be considerably under the influence of the syndicate, but he believed him honest. Bast and his two companions had put themselves in a highly uncomplimentary light, no matter how glib their explanations might be. It was certainly a stroke of luck that Smith had taken that comprehensive glance beneath the swinging door and entered by the rear.

"Just what the heck were you hombres fixin' tuh do?" the sheriff growled.

The crouchers straightened, seemed about to turn, when—

"Is it a new kind of game?" Smith drawled.

That drawl! Bast and his men recognized it instantly, and their frames went tense.

"Put them pistols back where they belong," Hellman

snapped, his walrus mustache quivering ferociously. "It's a pretty how-de-do when a prominent citizen stands inside a saloon with a gun in his hand, waitin' tuh salivate some luckless jasper which is about tuh step in for a friendly drink! By cripes, I got a good notion tuh jail you, Bast."

"You better pipe low, Hellman, if yuh expect tuh wear that star after next election. It's about time you learned what side of your bread's got the buter on it!" Bast snarled. "An' as fer me waitin' tuh salivate anybody— why, that's a laff! We're givin' a amachure play out tuh the Big 3 next week an' was in here practicin' up."

Smith grinned.

But there was no mirth on the lawman's stern countenance. "A likely tale," he said, putting a deal of skepticism into his tone. "A very likely tale. Turn around there, you two, an' quit edgin' toward them doors. Turn around an' let's have a squint at your pans."

Reluctantly, Bast's gun-slingers turned around.

"Huh! Newcomers tuh this neck of the woods, ain't yuh? I don't recollect seein' you before."

"A couple of new men Brux hired last week," Bast explained, eyeing the sheriff ominously. "You got no cause to be actin' proddy, Hellman. You're exceedin' your authority."

"I'm the best judge of that. Anybody would be suspicious comin' into a public place an' findin' three hombres standin' like I found you three," Hellman said softly. "I got nothing against the syndicate personally, understand, but I don't mind sayin' that this town is gettin' a mite fed up with Big 3 dominance. It ain't improvin' business any. You fellas better try steppin' soft an' easy for a spell."

"Is that a threat?" Bast growled.

"The cards is dealt; read 'em any was that suits your fancy."

Tiny flecks of fire appeared in the syndicate man's pale eyes. His breathing sounded harsh in the sudden silence and a vein throbbed visibly on his forehead. "Got anything more yuh feel like gettin' off yore chest?"

"Only this," said Hellman, standing firm; "buckwackers will operate at their own risk while I'm sheriffin' this county. Them that's caught will be strung up pronto to the handiest limb!" And, turning on his heel, the lawman left the saloon in a profound hush.

Smith grinned; it began to look as though the worm had turned. Ordering a drink, he said the bartender: "You better warn your boss that excitement of an emotional nature is bad for what ails him."

Bast's face went livid.

"How's the cow business?" Smith chuckled. "Been havin' any more fires lately?"

Malignant, baffled fury shone from Bast's pale eyes. There were strange noises in his throat and his big hands were clenching and unclenching spasmodically. He had all the ear-marks of a man primed for a killing.

His men looked at him questioningly, waiting for orders. But none came; Bast dared to do nothing further at the moment—the sheriff's grim warning was still ringing in his ears. With a hoarse snarl, he went striding toward one of the private rooms in the rear, Flynn and Harmon following.

Leaving the Tall Bottle, several moments later, Smith headed for the bank building. Not that he saw much use in visiting Timothy Klain, attorney for the syndicate; still, one never knew. There was always the possibility that Klain and the Big 3 might be on the outs at the moment. So thinking, he climbed the stairs and entered the lawyer's office.

Klain was a pompous, fat little fellow who wheezed at the least exertion. Taking the expensive cigar from his mouth, he gave his caller a cold, uncompromising stare.

"Well, whatever you're trying to sell, I don't want any," he wheezed. "I'm a busy man! I don't care to buy any books—legal or otherwise. I've more books than I know what to do with now. Never read 'em. I'm not interested in buying stock in mythical dams, new-fangled ways of branding cattle, or collapsible barns! You can't interest me in national advertising!

"If there is anything else that you care to see me about, speak quick—my time is highly valuable!"

"I bet if you put that on a phonograph record, it would sell like hot cakes," Smith chuckled. "What I want to see you about is some legal work."

"Then why didn't you say so?" snapped the lawyer testily. "I'm not a mind-reader, young man. What sort of legal work do you wish me to undertake?"

"I want to start slander proceedin's against the Big 3 syndicate."

"You—uh—you *what?*"

"Want you to start slander proceedin's for me against the Big 3," Smith repeated.

Timothy Klain blinked rapidly, bounced off his swivel chair and drew his paunchy self to his full five-feet-three. "If that is a joke, young man, I am not the person to play it on. Kindly take yourself out of my office without further delay!"

"Merry Christmas," said Smith, "an' a happy New Year in the hot place," and closed the door on the outside. "That bag of wind ain't for Smilin' Smith," he muttered as he clumped his way down the stairs. "I guess the Big 3 owns pretty much of the law in this part of the country, an' them as don't like it is free tuh move out."

Not long after Bast and the syndicate foreman set off for town, Jud Dixon saddled a horse and jogged townward himself. There were a number of things that needed tending, and Dixon was not the man to put off until tomorrow anything that could be done today.

No telling what that blundering fool of a Bast was up to! He was afraid to let the man out of his sight for fear he would bring all his plans and hopes to naught.

Dixon knew that Smith and his housekeeper had gone to town this morning for he had seen them pass about half an hour before Bast and Potak had started townward. There was no guessing the possible results from a meeting of those four. Such likely results as came unbidden to Dixon's mind were unpleasant, from his point of view. The Law must be kept on the Big 3 side of the fence at all cost!

There was a dark plan percolating through the sinister byways of Dixon's mind as he jogged along the dusty trail. A plan by which even yet he might gain the upper hand in the struggle with the yellow-haired outlander who had squatted on the Smithers place, like a leech on a bather's foot.

There was only one drawback; the plan involved Al Bast—an extremely unreliable quantity. Nevertheless, it was a plan capable of bringing about highly satisfying results, if things went through without hitch. Dixon was on his way to Bucksnort to make sure that they did so.

He wondered what the dude had found worth discussing with Bast the previous afternoon—for he had observed the conversation between the two among the pinons. Also he wondered what information Monahan had withheld from himself in order that he might privately sell it to Bast. But the solution of these puzzles eluded him, but served to widen the breach between himself and his blundering, head-strong partner.

Abruptly Dixon pulled his horse to a halt and sat staring at a second hoseman who blocked his way as he came jogging around a bend. The second rider was Monahan, and there was a hard grin on the dude's thin lips.

"Afternoon, Dixon. Kind of dusty, ain't it?"

"What the heck are you doing blocking the road like this?" Dixon demanded angrily.

"I been waitin' here since last night to have a word with you—that is, I been hangin' around nearby. I want to sell you some information."

"I ain's passin' out hundred dollar banknotes this afternoon." Dixon grunted. "Better save your information for Al Bast—seems like you an' him are gettin' right chummy."

"Nope," Monahan shook his head. "I sold Bast this information yesterday afternoon. I got reason to think he didn't pass it on to you. You'd be interested in it. Better pull out your wallet."

"I'm not buyin' second-hand information," Dixon said, then stopped. After all, if Monahan had already sold this information to Bast, perhaps he had better learn what it was. He could not afford to have his hot-tempered partner —Dixon broke his thoughts off there and eyeing Monahan suspiciously asked:

"What is the information about?"

"Smith's housekeeper—that Dolores dame."

Dixon grunted. "Jesse James never had anything on you," he said sourly. "How much are you figgerin' to make me pay for your stale news?"

"Make it an even hundred an' I'll give you the works."

Dixon counted out some money and put it in Monahan's outstretched hand. "Get busy, Judas, an' start talkin'," he growled.

The dude from Texas grinned brazenly. "I held out a little on Bast," he said. "I told him he better get a squint of what's inside that locket the dame wears on a gold chain around her neck. I told him there was a coupla pictures in it. But I didn't admit I knew whose they were. I got a look at 'em night 'fore last though, an' there's one of 'em you'll recognize without much difficulty—"

"Go back to the Big 3 line camp an' wait for me," Dixon snapped. "I got to talk with you again, later. But right now I'm in a hurry. Get the hell out of my way!" And with a sinister glint in his bright-button eyes, the rancher went spurring down the trail toward town, for he could guess whose picture was in that locket and had no intention of letting Bast ruin his plans a second time.

Unfortunately, Monahan *had* told Bast whose pictures were in the locket, and even as Dixon went hurrying toward town, Bast, in the back room of the Tall Bottle, was laboriously penning a letter.

"Wait till they get this at the S-Bar-S," he growled to Flynn and Harmon as he flung aside his pen and sealed the letter in an envelope. "That slat-sided, grinnin' chessy-cat of a Smith'll sing another tune!" He handed it to Flynn. "Take that right over to the Post Office, Lefty. Here's a jolt that'll catch that yeller-haired joker beneath the belt!"

"Hadn't yuh better wait till Potak brings yuh the locket?" Harmon asked. "Mebbe that damn dude was lyin' to yuh."

"What's the difference? Lie or not, the result is bound tuh be the same—as far as the girl's concerned."

Warned by some deep instinct or subtle intuition—perhaps by some trifling difference in the light by which she was regarding the storekeeper's supply of merchandise—Dolores suddenly whirled about to stare behind her. There in the doorway, framed against the sunlight streaming in about him, stood black Potak, a smearing grin on his handsome, dark-skinned face.

The girl's hands crept to her breast, perhaps to still the sudden throbbing of her heart. But though her face paled, her eyes remained defiant.

"Hello, kitten," Potak chuckled as he moved inside to lean against the wall. "Long time I no see you, *niña*. Gonna give me that kiss we was talkin' about three-four weeks ago?"

"Go away, *señor*. I have no kees to give away."

"Shucks, *querida,* that ain't no way to talk to yore pinin' caballero," Potak's grin widened as he twisted the waxed ends of his pointed, black mustache. "Come, come! A *mestiza* wench like you should be glad of a white man's attentions."

"One big lie!" Dolores cried with flashing eyes. "I am

no *mestiza!* Have a care how you talk to me. *Señor* Smeeth will—"

Potak laughed. "Hell, that *cabrillo* won't be botherin' me or anyone else again," he sneered. " 'Cause why? 'Cause right now he's gettin' rubbed out down at the Tall Bottle!" and he guffawed coarsely.

The girl's pale face went white as ashes. One hand flew to her lips to stifle the cry that rose; not for herself, but for the man she loved. Could this thing be true? She shivered as she saw the gloating light in Potak's evil eyes.

He strode toward her and she backed away, one hand held out before her as though to fend him off. "Keep away —keep away from me or, Mother of God, I weel use my knife!"

But she was not swift enough for him.

Potak sprang even as she reached for it. His right arm snaked out and his hand fastened on the neck of her blouse. With a savage jerk he ripped it open to the waist. The knife thudded to the floor and stuck there quivering. The next moment he had her in his arms and was covering her with slobbering kisses. She clawed and kicked and struggled, and he laughed.

One of his hands went abruptly to her throat, while he held her with his other. A swift jerk sufficed to snap the golden locket from its tiny chain. He thrust it in a pocket of his vest and laughed coarsely as he kissed her again.

"*Sangre de Dios!*" she sobbed, and clawed at his face with her clenched fingers. When they came away there were bloody lines on his face and the grinning leer was gone.

"You danged little gutter rat!" he swore, and struck her with his fist.

As she reeled backward, the storekeeper rushed forward. "God in heaven!" he screamed. "Would you kill her?"

Potak jerked a black-butted gun from its holster. As

the storekeeper rushed at him he swung it once. He dropped and did not move.

The cowman strode to the girl's side, stooped and yanked her to her feet. Her eyes snapped with fury.

"Pelado! Maldito!" she panted as she struggled to break his grip.

"Hold still, dang yuh!" he snarled. With a vicious movement he twisted her arms behind her back till her face went taut and the tears came into her eyes. He licked his lips as he looked at her.

But his wiry form went rigid as, behind him, a cold voice drawled:

"That's enough, polecat—turn around."

•

CHAPTER XVII

Buzzard Bait

LIKE a cat swapping ends, Potak spun as he heard that hated drawl, and his clawing hands went plunging hipward.

Smiling Smith took a long step forward and, throwing the whole weight of his upper body behind the blow, struck Potak on the jaw. The foreman's head jerked sideways and his black-butted weapons slid back in their scarred holsters as, beneath that fearful blow, Potak's wiry form went reeling backward.

The Smiler went right after him, and there was no mirth in the grin that spread his lips. The big foreman recovered his balance and tried to cover. Snarling vicious curses, he backed away, his bloodshot eyes twin slits of blazing fury.

Suddenly he threw all caution to the winds. Lowering his head he charged, his big fists swinging like striking hammers, jolting Smith like bullets each time they scored a hit.

But the Smiler seemed immune to pain.

Back and forth across the cluttered floor they swayed, snarling, kicking, slugging.

Presently Potak thought he saw a chance and went lunging for his guns again. But—

"Get them paws up, polecat!" Smith thrust the words out through his teeth. "I'm gonna take your works apart an' see what makes yuh tick! Get them paws up, dang yuh!"

Smith lunged forward with the words. Desperately Potak raised his arms to shield his face. Smith struck him in the midriff, a jolting, short-arm blow. Potak's arms went down to his abdomen and a sobbing grunt was wrung from his snarling lips. He doubled over as he fought for breath. An uppercut straightened him and a flashing left caught him in the mouth, smashing him backward.

Again and again the Smiler struck, ripping, smashing blows that battered the dark-skinned face before him and covered it with blood.

Sobbing with rage, Potak lowered his head and charged again, arms flailing like the blades of a windmill. Smith stepped aside and as the big man passed, slapped him on the back of the head with his open palm. The foreman cursed and whirled.

Toe to toe they stood and slugged, grueling, jolting blows that never missed.

Then suddenly Potak's booted foot came up, caught Smith in the stomach. Even as his body cramped, a pile-driver blow smashed against his chest, hurling him backward, sending him sprawling on his back three feet away.

A hoarse growl of triumph broke from Potak's battered lips and drowned Dolores' scream. The Big 3 foreman saw his chance and took it; his hands swept down to leather.

The girl sprang forward, striving to hold down those lifting wrists. With a snarl, Potak flung her aside and reached again. But Smith was up now and lurching toward

136

him. Even as the black-butted guns swung free of leather, Smith, summoning his last reserve of strength, sent his right fist smashing beneath the foreman's jaw. With a sobbing, gasping intake of breath Black Potak reeled away; his sagging knees let go and spilled him on the floor.

Smith staggered to his side and kicked the guns from his loosened grasp, sending them spinning across the room. As he stood there swaying above his fallen enemy, Dolores came to him with a little cry and put her arms about him.

Presently Smith put the girl aside and, having somewhat recovered his strength, sliced a bit of rope from a great ball of it on the counter and lashed Potak's wrists and ankles securely. When he had finished, Dolores stooped above the Big 3 foreman and swiftly searched his pockets. With a glad cry she stood up, the locket in her hand.

"What's that?" Smith asked indifferently.

"My locket, your honor. Potak stole it from me before you came. See," she opened it and held it toward him, "My blessed mother and my father."

Smith looked at the tiny pictured faces in the locket. One was a dark-eyed señorita, in looks not unlike the girl beside him. There was a Spanish comb in her high-piled midnight hair.

"Is she not beautiful, señor?"

Smith nodded; he was staring at the other picture and there was a bleak expression on his countenance. The young-appearing face of the man in the faded picture, with its sharp little eyes staring out from the sleepy lids, its gimlet mouth and sharp features, was not unfamiliar to Smiling Smith. He looked hard and long, trying to persuade himself that there was some mistake, but knew there was not. The face of the man in the locket was the face of Dan Jalnor, alias Si Jones, the one-time Bucksnort banker!

"What ees wrong, eh?" Dolores asked, noting his grim

expression as she pulled the torn blouse closed about her shoulders.

"Did you ever live in El Paso, *niña?*"

"Si, we lived there, my mother an' I, long time ago. Then she died and I ran away, for I wanted to see the world."

"And your father—do you remember him?"

Dolores shook her head and the sunlight played in her locks. "He died when I was very small, I think." She regarded him curiously, her deep brown eyes both soft and soulful, a touch of color in her cheeks.

Smith was thinking fast. It was plain he would have to go to Juarez and seek this Don Anastacio Escobar, this Mexican judge who was Dolores' grandfather. He—

"Of what ees your honor thinking?" the girl broke in upon his thoughts. "Had we not better go away from here?"

Smith roused himself. "Yeah, we better be gettin' away." He noticed that the proprietor was beginning to show signs of recovering consciousness. "How did he get that nasty cut?"

"He was trying to help me an' that Potak hit heem with hees gun. He mus' do something for heem, no?"

Smith nodded and got some water for her from a pail behind the counter. With a piece of goods torn from a bolt nearby, Dolores bathed the storekeeper's wound and presently he opened his eyes and sat up. He seemed dazed as he sat there holding his head in his hands.

Smith got a pair of burlap bags from somewhere and placed the girl's bundles and packages in them, slung the sacks across his shoulder and carried them out to the hitch rail where Flea-Bite and Dolores' horse were tethered.

When Smith and the girl left the store a short time later, Dolores was wearing a leather riding skirt and a suede jacket had replaced her torn blouse. Smith turned their horses toward the Post Office. He wished to see if Crane had written him yet.

Dolores waited with the horses while he went inside the bleached frame building.

There were, he found, two letters waiting for the S-Bar-S. Neither was from Crane. One was for Dolores, and was postmarked Bucksnort, 4:15. Smith glanced at the clock. It was now almost five. Kind of odd, he thought, and put the letter in his pocket.

Then he opened the envelope addressed to himself. It was from the man who had sold him the three carloads of sheep derailed by the syndicate at Big Bend trestle. The sheepman was advising him that his last payment was due in three days' time.

Smith scowled as he left the building. Unless he could get hold of Crane very soon, he might not even have a ranch, let alone the price of the final payment on some sheep he did not have!

He thought it rather odd that Crane hadn't sent him the title or deed to the Smithers place. The fellow had had ample time to realize that the deed was still in his possession. "Some people," Smith muttered, "jest ain't got any consideration for other folks at all!"

He stepped up to Flea-Bite and swung into the saddle. Then he remembered the letter addressed to the girl and, fishing it from his pocket, handed it to her.

"Some love-lorn hombre's been writin' you a billey-do, I reckon."

Dolores looked surprised, but did not open her unexpected letter. Plainly her interest was all centered in Smiling Smith. They looked at each other and smiled.

"I got to take a trip right soon," Smith said. "I'll likely be gone a day or two. But as soon as I get back, *niña,* you an' me is goin' to get hitched up!"

What a sparkle came to Dolores' dusky eyes! What a radiant glow suffused her cheeks! But they were still in town so she contented herself with tightly squeezing his hand where it rested on the pommel. Then suddenly she felt him stiffen; she followed his staring gaze. A man was just dismounting before the Tall Bottle saloon several doors down the street. As he started up the steps, Dolores turned to Smith.

"Who is thees man who makes you look so strange?"

"That's Dixon," he answered grimly, "one of the Big Three—in fact, the brains of the outfit. He's the most dangerous man in the county, *niña*. Come, it's time we were headin' home."

As they reached the outskirts of town and were about to swing onto the trail that led toward Smithers Valley, the Smiler stopped their horses. A rider was coming toward them. It was Trigger Willmoth. Smith's face paled at sight of him.

"What's gone wrong?" he demanded gruffly when Willmoth stopped his horse beside them.

"Nary a thing, boss. Me an' Tranter ran out of chewin' so I volunteered tuh come in after some. Say," his eyes lighted up as he studied Dolores' flushed and happy features, "yuh shore looks pretty as a little red wagon, Miss Dolo, ma'am. That's a right becomin' outfit yuh got on."

"Gracias, señor," she thanked him.

"There's chewin' in one of these sacks, Willmoth," Smith said abruptly. "I got to go back tuh town; I'm leavin' for El Paso tonight, if I can get a train. You take these sacks an' Dolores back tuh the ranch. An' stay inside the valley till I get back. I'll probably be back tomorrow night; leastways, I'm hopin' to. You take right good care of Dolo—she's goin' tuh be Mrs. Smilin' Smith when I get home."

Leaving his flea-bitten nag in Jed Kallis' stable, Smith strode down the street toward the railroad depot, a large frame shack that was painted red.

His main reason for making this trip was to ascertain whether or not Dan Jalnor, the crooked ex-mayor of El Paso, had ever married Dolores' mother. Not that it made any difference to Smiling Smith, but he thought it might mean a lot to the girl, should she ever be so unfortunate as to find out about the affair, which he hoped with all his heart she would not.

He wondered if Monahan suspected that Dolores was the late Bucksnort banker's daughter. Probably not, he reflected. Monahan had not seemed to know whether Jalnor's child was a boy or a girl. And Jones, he thought sardonically, had never even suspected that he had a child, and certainly he could not have known that his daughter was in Bucksnort. The ways of Fate were inscrutable.

As he strode on toward the frame building that housed the Bucksnort depot, dusk was settling swiftly on the town. And behind him, partially hidden by the evening shadows, stole a pair of stealthy figures—men in high-heeled boots with holsters sagging at their thighs.

Smith learned from the depot master that a train for El Paso would be in at seven-forty-five. He looked at his watch and found that he had but ten minutes to wait. As he sat down on one of the long benches that lined the depot walls, he did not notice that two scowling faces were covertly watching him through the window at his side. In fact, the Smiler at that moment was too busy with his thoughts to notice anything.

After sitting there awhile, he got up and approached the ticket-seller's window, where he purchased a round-trip ticket to El Paso.

"Looks like you been in a fight, Mister," the man grinned as he handed Smith a thin piece of pink pasteboard and his change. "Did yuh manage to hit the other fella any?"

"I sorta nicked him once or twice," Smith answered. "I reckon I do look a mite scary. Got any place around here where I can wash off some of the marks o' battle?"

"Sure thing, this is a up-to-date station . . . go right over there to that door marked 'Gents.' You'll probably find one or two paper towels inside. We had quite a supply there yesterday, but the kids has been makin' hats out of 'em. Anyways, you can always use the roller towel on the back of the door."

After the Smiler had to some extent remedied his rough appearance, he returned to the bench by the window and sat down. It was quite dark outside, now, he saw. Then his thoughts turned to Dolores and his eyes took on a far-away expression.

He thought of her big brown eyes, so deep and soft and soulful, and of her lithe and willowy figure, that somehow reminded him of a rose, it seemed so delicate and fragile.

He smiled as he recalled the delight with which she had received his presents—the suede jacket and leather riding skirt and the new scarf to twine about her tawny hair.

He sighed. It seemed impossible that she could love him. What had he to offer such a very marvel of a girl, he asked himself? That he found no answer is not surprising, for few men do on such occasions.

Of course, he reflected presently, Smiling Smith—two-firsted man of action—had no business getting married to anybody! He was not the marrying type! But, at last awoke to the fact that he really was in love with her and she with him, marriage seemed the only sensible solution. It was odd he had not thought of it before!

The distant whistle of his train roused him from his roving thoughts. He got up and strolled to the window and, pressing his nose against the dusty glass, looked out. Yep! there is came; snorting, smoking, grumbling. He went outside and when it had screeched to a snorting stop, got himself aboard and found a seat beside a window.

There were not many folks at the station tonight to meet the train, he decided, peering out. Only two in sight. One of them was coming toward the train, toward the very car in which he sat. There was a sort of familiar look about the fellow, Smith thought absently. It was pretty dark to make out faces, though. There were lights on the train, so

it seemed likely enough that the two men outside had recognized him, if they knew him.

Hmm. Where had that first fellow gone? The one who
had been approaching his car? The other man was drawing near, now, he noticed.

"Tickets, please!"

Smith looked up to find a conductor with a red face
standing in the aisle. There was only one man besides
Smith passengering this particular car, so while the conductor punched the other man's ticket, Smith fumbled in
his pockets for his own and when, presently, he found it
he stuck it in the band of his Stetson. Then he turned his
attention once again to the platform outside the window.

The second man was standing quite close to the car and
—Hell!

Smith suddenly stiffened. The fellow was drawing a gun!

Smith's attention was diverted momentarily as the conductor reached for the ticket in his hat band. After punch-
ing a vicious hole in the inoffensive pasteboard, the conductor handed it back to Smith, who replaced it in his hat,
then once again pressed his face to the window at his side.

He suddenly realized with an unpleasant prickling of
the scalp that the man with the gun was Jud Dixon. And
that Dixon was pointing his gun toward the very window
in which Smith sat.

"Hey, you fool!" he shouted. "Cut it out! This ain't no
time for jokes."

Dixon shouted something, too, but Smith couldn't make
out the words. Then a spurt of orange flame lashed from
the muzzle of Dixon's gun. *Crash! Crash! Crash!* The
muted explosions were plainly audible even though the
train was moving, slowly gathering headway. With a
tinkle of shattered glass, a hole appeared in the window
at Smith's side.

Great guns! Was the fellow crazy? Smith sprang to his
feet in swift alarm.

Dixon was shouting again and Smith could hear the

words now, due perhaps to that sinister hole in the window:

"Dang you Smith, for a murderin' hound!" Dixon was bellowing, his hard-chiseled features distorted with rage. "You ain't goin' tuh get away with it this time!" Again the pistol belched; again and yet again, and three more holes appeared as though by magic in the window of the train as Smith threw himself flat in the aisle.

Came the pound of running feet as Smith picked himself up from the aisle and glanced hastily out the shattered window. The lights of Bucksnort were fading swiftly rearward as the Limited picked up steam.

"Whew!" Smith wiped cold sweat from his forehead and turned to find out who was shaking him so unpleasantly. It was the red-faced conductor. "What the heck you up to?" the man in the uniform growled. "Don't you know it's against the law tuh shoot holes in the windows of this train?"

"I wish you'd explain that to the hombre that done the shootin'," Smith muttered. "I hope yuh don't think I enjoy playin' substitute for a target!"

"Do you mean to say somebody on the station platform did that shooting?" the conductor eyed him incredulously.

"Well, if yuh find any gun in this car, yuh can blame it on me," Smith said, and meant it.

"That's right," said the other man in Smith's car, who was sitting further back. "This fellow didn't do no shooting. It was somebody outside, and it looked to me as though they were trying to salivate this fellow."

Smith cast a look at the speaker and saw that he was a drummer of some sort in a brown derby hat. "Thanks, friend," Smith grinned. "Hope I can do as much for you some time."

"By jingoes, I hope you won't have no occasion to," the man shivered. "I'd call that a pretty close shave."

CHAPTER XVIII

The Die Is Cast

As the train roared through the mountainous country of southern New Mexico, the Smiler—having changed his seat—sat humped over like a bent pin. There was a deep scowl between his eyes and an expression of mighty concentration on his bronzed, hard-bitten face.

From time to time he rubbed his lean jaw reflectively—but all to no avail. He could not sift out a plausible reason why, if Jud Dixon had wanted to shoot him, he had not chosen a less public spot for his attempted homicide. His every action on the depot platform had been at variance with what Smith knew of the man's cautious, scheming nature.

"Damnation!" he snorted finally in disgust. Here, surely, was a problem of such complexity as to rival the ancient riddle of the Sphinx!

With a sigh, he composed himself to sleep. Not that he was tired, particularly, but he saw no sense in staying awake when it would be at least four hours before the speeding train chugged into its destination.

Smith arrived in El Paso shortly after 1:00 A.M.

Leaving the station in a horse-drawn hack, he had himself driven directly to the Texan side of the old toll bridge entering Juarez. There he got out, paid his driver and set out afoot across the Rio Grande. At the toll house, he paid his fee and exchanged bantering words with the uniformed attendant anent the latter's resemblance to a certain *Señor* James.

After some time he found himself on a brilliantly lighted street. Along both sides of this were saloons, tourist shops, gambling dens and dance halls. The tourist shops outnumbered the rest about four to one, Smith noted, but at this hour were closed and dark. And then to his left he saw a white-washed adobe building on whose front wall was painted in large purple letters,

KING DAN'S CANTINA

"It's a cinch it wouldn't be any use callin' on Dan Anastacio at this unholy hour," he muttered. "Reckon I might as well pass some time in this dump—an' here's hoping it's a peaceful place."

Entering, he was met by an elegant Mexican in dress suit who conducted him to a little table along one side of a hardwood dance floor. An orchestra was blaring for all it was worth and gliding couples filled the floor. The place was illuminated with colored Japanese lanterns strung on wires about a foot below the plastered ceiling. One glance about the dim-lit room was enough to convince Smiling Smith that King Dan's Cantina was conducted for tourist trade from the States. The only thing Mexican about it were the waiters and its locality.

He grinned sardonically when the waiter left with his order for wine, "I better not linger in this place," he told himself. "Too high-toned for a trouble-pestered cowpoke like me."

Looking about him curiously he found that no one in the long room wore range clothes but himself. There were evening gowns and tuxedoes, dress suits and business suits, but no high-heeled boots and ten gallon hats save those in his possession. Plainly Smiling Smith was out of his element.

The Mexican waiter had hardly brought his bottle of *vino* before a slight commotion became manifest at the far end of the rom, close by the orchestra which was now enjoying a well-earned intermission. All about the scene of the disturbance, people were rising from their chairs. Some looked alarmed, some curious, but all appeared to be interested.

Smith could see a burly man with an iron-gray beard in angry altercation with a well-dressed Mexican with a scar across one cheek. The latter was gesticulating frantically. Abruptly his left hand swept inside his dinner jacket and came out with a long-bladed knife.

Like a whirlwind the burly, bearded American was upon him. The knife flew in one direction, and its owner flew in another to land sprawled-out and still upon the floor.

In an instant the place was in an uproar; screams, curses and shouts resounding on every side as the patrons sprang from their seats and, propelling their women before them, went rushing for the exits.

The burly American seemed in no great hurry. He even turned for a final look at the man who had tried to stab him.

Smith's tall, gaunt frame went rigid, his fists clenched till their knuckles shone like lumps of ice. He stared again at the man across the room. The world began a dizzy spin as he table like a man in the grip of paralysis, still staring at the like a man in the grip of paralysis, still staring at the bearded man across the hardwood floor. Then, as the burly American sprang toward an open window, Smith came to life with a loud:

"Crane!"

But the American paid no attention and an instant later he vanished outside the handy window.

With a great oath, Smith went into action. He waded through the crowd endeavoring to leave the cantina via the front entrance like a gridiron hero plunging desperately with the ball.

Elbowing the last scurrying person from his path, he took out after the bearded man at a hard run. He felt no small interest in the cause of the fellow's quarrel, but felt it highly desirable to overtake the fleeing figure. For the burly man was Crane, the star-toter who had sold him the Smithers place and neglected to give him the deed!

The fugitive proved to be a marvelous sprinter despite his weight. Smith was hard put to even keep his quarry in sight. More than once as he pursued his fellow American around dim-lit corners and down shadowy alleys through evil-smelling refuse, he cursed his tight-fitting high-heeled boots that caused his feet new misery at every bounding step.

Ahead, some distance to the left, Smith abruptly spied a narrow doorway in a wall that flanked the sidewalk. At the same moment he realized that Crane was making for it. He redoubled his efforts but the fugitive was first to reach the door and pass through, slamming it behind him.

The Smiler wasted no time in learning if the barrier was locked. He took a running jump, caught the top of the wall with his hands and pulled himself up. Across a tiny courtyard, centered by a gurgling fountain, he saw Crane letting himself out a door in the opposite wall. Smith let out a yell like the screech of a catamount and called on the fugitive to stop. But this, Crane declined to do and swiftly vanished through the door.

When Smith passed out the door he saw that the burly American had gained another fifty yards. Down a dusty lane he led the way, the Smiler pounding behind him breathing oaths and threats and entreaties. Through a maze of crooked alleys, dark and evil-smelling, the pursuer floundered, finally pulling up with a disgusted snort. Somewhere in this shadowy labyrinth Crane had disappeared. Smith had found the star-toter but to lose him.

Smith was in a sour mood when around eleven o'clock he found himself near the board-walled arena in which the citizens of Jaurez were wont to hold their bull-fights of a Sunday afternoon.

All morning he had been tramping hither and yon in continued search for the elusive Crane. But no success had crowned his efforts. A glance at his watch told him that it was high time he set out to find the residence of old Don Anastacio Escobar, grandfather of Dolores.

The home of the retired judge, when Smith found it, proved to be the very place whose walled yard he had dashed through the night before in swearing chase of the bearded American who had scared the patrons from their pleasant pastimes in the cantina of King Dan.

Don Anastacio Escobar had once been a tall man, but now his aged frame was stooped and shrunken. His cheeks were hollow and wrinkled and the faded eyes beneath his shaggy white brows were vague. He wore a bolero jacket and the shirt beneath it was well-made and of white silk. He wore dark limb-clutching velvet trousers, striped with red along the seams. When his guest had introduced himself and he had sent his servants for wine and cakes, the old man seated himself wearily.

"It is long, *Señor* Smith, since I have had visitors. My manners you will find, perhaps, are no longer of the best. I tire easily these days, alas, so perhaps you will be so kind as to inform me now in what manner I may be of use to you."

"You once had a daughter, I believe, who married an unscrupulous jasper what was mayor of El Jaso—until he skipped out with the city funds," Smith began, and paused.

The old Don's wrinkled face had darkened, his bony, olive-skinned hands had tightened on the arms of his chair. A fierce light of hatred flared up in his faded eyes, but swiftly vanished. He looked at his visitor with new interest.

"Yes," he said. "I once had such a daughter."

"I come from your grand-daughter, Dolores Jalnor," Smith spoke softly.

"From Dolores? From little Dolores?" The Don's old eyes grew misty. "He comes from Dolores," he whispered, falteringly, wonderingly, as though there were cause to doubt. He half rose from his chair, then relaxed as though exhausted.

"You amaze me, *señor*." His tone had become cold and formal.

"It's the truth. She and I are to be married tomorrow. I came to let you know."

"And why," asked the old man, "did you think I would be interested?"

"She's your granddaughter, isn't she?"

"She is the child of my daughter who married the gringo, Jalnor, against my wishes," Don Anastacio said slowly. "I have never quite forgiven Florita.

"And Dolores ran away from me one night after her mother died. Ran away, so her note said, to see the world for herself—and she a child of nine. Well, has she seen it?"

Smith could find no words with which to answer, and the old man spoke again:

"Staying with that old thief of a father, I suppose, eh?"

"No. It happens that Jalnor was a resident of Bucksnort," Smith said slowly, "but Dolores never knew he was her father. He was murdered the other night."

"A fitting end for him," the ex-judge's voice was bleak.

The servant returned at that moment with cakes and wine which he placed on a low table at Don's right hand. Pouring out two glasses of the sparkling ruby liquid, the man handed one to the guest and the other to his master and silently withdrew.

Don Anastacio suddenly smiled and lifted his glass. "Tell me," he said, "is she pretty, this runaway Dolores?"

"Pretty?" Smith snorted. "Why she's the most beautiful gal in New Mexico!"

The old Don nodded. "Her mother, too, was beautiful. She had eyes like limpid pools at dusk."

There was silence for a time, and presently they lifted their glasses to each other and smiled. "For both of you, *señor,* I wish the happiness. You must come again to see me, you and the little Dolores."

Leaving Don Anastacio's, Smith flagged a Mexican cab driver and told him that he wished to be driven to the Juarez side of the toll bridge into El Paso and they started off.

When he arrived at the station in El Paso, the train was just starting its wheezing and snorting way. Smiler lowered his head and started pumping his arms and legs in a mad dash. He caught it, but only by a flying leap.

"Whew!" he muttered, panting, and headed for the smoker. He got the door open, then froze on the threshold, staring. There were four men inside and they were playing cards.

"Well, blast my soul!" Smith growled, and strode inside.

The man facing him was Crane!

In the Sheriff's office at Bucksnort, shortly after the train pulled out that was carrying the boss of the S-Bar-S toward El Paso, Dan Hellman sat scowling at Jud Dixon. "Let's hear that yarn again," he said, at last. "I wanta get it straight. No chance of a slip-up, eh? You're sure it was Smith?"

Dixon stood there solidly, bulking large in the sheriff's small, bare office, his hard-chiseled countenance a grim and somber mask.

"There's no chance of a slip-up, Dan. I saw the dang skunk do it, I tell yuh! He was sittin' by a window facin' the platform in the next to the last car. As Bast ran forward, Smith pulled a gun and shot through the window just as the train started. Bast fell at the first shot. . . . It's plain downright murder, Sheriff!"

"Where was you?" Hellman asked after thinking over the other's words. "Where was you standin' when Smith fired an' Big Al fell?"

"I was standin' by the door to the depot, wonderin' what Bast was aimin' tuh talk with Smith about. As Bast fell, I yanked my six-gun an' unloosed some lead. I peppered the window where Smith was settin' but he ducked soon as Al went down. The most cold-blooded killin' I ever see." Dixon muttered huskily.

"Well, I'll get in touch with the surroundin' towns an' telegraph the neighborin' counties to be on the lookout for him. It's a cinch he'll be gettin' off that train at the first likely-lookin' spot—"

"Hold on," Dixon growled. "I ain't so sure of that. He may be pullin' out of the country altogether. On the other hand, he may be aimin' to come back here again in a few days if he thinks I haven't talked and am aiming to settle with him private."

No readable expression was on the sheriff's face as he stared at the Big 3 man. "What are you hintin' at?"

Dixon chewed his underlip thoughtfully. "I was thinkin', Dan, it might be a good idea to sort of lie low awhile. Don't let news of the killin' out. It might be that Smith will get the notion somehow that he ain't suspicioned an' come back. In fact, I'm almost certain he'll be back— don't forget that dame he's sweet on, that Dolores kid that's supposed to be his housekeeper."

"I thought him an' her got married."

"They haven't yet, but I believe they're intendin' to. That's the main reason why I'm certain he'll be back."

"An' you suggest that we wait an' see, is that it?"

Dixon nodded. "If he comes back, we can let him get to the ranch without suspectin'. Then we can swear in a posse of my men an' go out there an' get him and that rustlin' Tranter, both. That's the sensible thing to do."

"It may look that way to you, Mister, but I ain't so sure—"

"You ain't sure of gettin' elected into the sheriff's office again, either—without my help," Dixon pointed out with a faint smile.

Crane looked up as Smith strode into the smoker like some great Tom-cat about to pounce. A grin parted his bearded lips. "Wal, if it ain't the new boss of Smithers Valley! Long time no see you, *amigo!*"

"You coulda seen me last night," Smith growled, "if you hadn't been in such a whale of a hurry tuh lose yourself after you left King Dan's. Cripes, I chased you over half of Juarez, I reckon, 'fore yuh finally gave me the slip!"

"Gosh, was that long-legged pelican you? . . . Wal, I wanta know! An' all the time I thought you was one of that greaser's gun-slingin' pardners! That's a joke on me, all right." Crane threw down his cards and cashed in. "Let's go some place where we can *habla* private-like," he suggested, and led the way to the observation car where they found seats to themselves on the rear platform.

For a time they watched the wasteland scenery flash past in silence. They were riding through a desert region wherein the distorted branches of Joshua trees were green against the hot white sky.

Crane shot a sidelong look at his companion, and suddenly his right hand described a forward-and-back motion that was faster than the eye could follow. When it stopped, there was a leveled sixgun in it—and the weapon's muzzle was pointed straight at Smiling Smith.

The Smiler half rose from his chair, and there was no smile upon his lips. The knuckles stood out whitely on his tight-clenched hands. His eyes were cold, with a gleam like polished metal.

"Take it easy," Crane warned softly. "No hand moves faster than a bullet."

Smith sank back in his chair. Carefully he produced the makings and built a brown-paper cigarette. He grinned, but the blue eyes above his Roman nose remained cold and hard as the metal of Crane's menacing pistol.

"Feelin' sort of proddy, ain't yuh?"

"That depends," said Crane. "I'm waitin' to hear your story."

"What story?"

"Your version of why yuh chased me all around Juarez last night. Start talkin'."

"I thought we was playin' tag an' I was it," Smith drawled sardonically.

"You almost was," Crane grunted. "Unfortunately, I

left the hotel without my gun. You was lucky. If I'd had it, yuh wouldn't be here now." A dry laugh crossed the bearded lips. "I'm givin' yuh two minutes tuh answer my question, Smith, an' yuh'd better answer—real serious-like."

Smith smiled thinly. "Why keep this farce up? You know durn well why I was follerin' you. I was after the deed tuh that ranch you sold me four-five weeks ago. I reckon you was playin' me for a sucker—" Smith suddenly broke off to stare at his companion.

Crane was staring at him strangely. Suddenly he swore. "Are you tellin' me the truth?"

"Take it or leave it."

The suspicion in Crane's narrowed eyes gave way to amazement. "An' you didn't have any connection with that Mex I knocked seat-over-eyebrows at King Dan's?"

"I don't know where you got that notion," Smith said dryly. "But yuh can throw it away—I sure didn't. I don't know the gent from Adam's off-ox."

"Wall, I'll be danged!"

"Yeah, I certainly hope so," Smith grunted as Crane returned his gun to leather. "You holdin' that deed out on me has sure caused me one awful load o' trouble."

"Wall, I'll be danged!" Crane said again, and laughed. "An' I been thinkin' you was connected with that dope ring I been after! Good Lord, fella, I forgot all about that deed—it plumb slipped my mind I been so dang busy lately. Yuh see I'm a—wal, I'm sorta connected with the government. I got a lot on my mind."

Reaching into his coat pocket, the bearded man produced a bunch of papers held together with an elastic band. Slipping the rubber off, he thumbed through them, finally pulling one from among its companions and handing it to Smith. "There yuh are," he chuckled. "There's yore missin' deed."

CHAPTER XIX

"DEATH TUH SMILIN' SMITH!"

WHEN Jud Dixon returned to the temporary headquarters of the Big 3 syndicate at the line-camp near the head of Grasshopper Draw, he was feeling fairly well pleased with the world in general and himself in particular. He had, in fact, forgotten all about telling Monahan that he would see him at the ranch when he returned from town. It was, therefore, with something of surprise that he beheld the dude sitting in the easiest chair with which the old shack was now equipped, smoking a fat cigar and swapping lies with Black Potak, who was more or less cut up and bruised about the face. Nearby sat Two-Word Brux, arms crossed and staring at the rafters in solemn contemplation.

They all looked round as Dixon entered.

"You're lookin' pleased as the cat that swallered the goldfish," Monahan commented.

Dixon made no answer but stared ominously at Potak. "What happened to you? Been playin' around that yeller-haired pelican from Smithers Valley again? . . . It's about time yuh learned to steer clear of him, I should think."

Potak snarled. "I'll fix that—"

"Yeah," Dixon interrupted dryly. "That's what Bast said. Smith shot him tonight in down. Shot him down without a chance, then lit out aboard a train."

A sudden silence descended on the room. Brux, Potak and Monahan stared at the speaker in silent wonder. In the yellow lamplight their faces looked like molded plaster masks. Potak was the first to speak, and oddly enough Bast's tragic end seemed to have left him unmoved. His mind was busy with the significance of Dixon's statement: "By gosh, we got that joker now!" A look of unholy joy lit up his face as he growled the words vindictively.

Dixon's eyes flickered strangely. "I think we have. I've persuaded the sheriff not to let out the information. Several people saw the corpse, but they don't know that Smith was the killer."

"Yuh mean tuh stand there an' say you're gonna let a chance like this slip out of our fingers? Cripes, yuh must be plumb outa yore head, Jud!" Potak cursed.

Dixon's smile was not pleasant. "You're like Bast used tuh be," he said coldly; "always poppin' off half-cocked. 'Course I ain't passin' up a chance like this. I'm just tryin' tuh fix it so there won't be any slip-up this time."

"I've got the sheriff muzzled so's he won't spill the beans. Why? 'Cause I'm pretty durn sure Smith'll be back in a coupla days. When he comes, I want him to get to Smithers Valley where he can hole up at his ranch."

His companions eyed him blankly.

The grimace on Dixon's face grew saturnine. "Hellman'll get a chance to serve warrants on two of that outfit, this way, Smith an' Tranter—Smith for murder an' Tranter for rustlin' Big 3 cattle. Hellman will have to ride by here to serve them warrants. An' with Smith holed up the way he'll be, the sheriff will have to swear in a posse so's tuh make sure he gets a chance tuh serve his papers. That's where *we* come in."

But it was plain the others didn't grasp this marvelous opportunity he had created. There was perplexity and bewilderment on the faces turned toward him, and a little anger, too.

"Cripes, what numbskulls I'm teamed up with!" Dixon's hard-chiseled features showed that his patience was wearing thin. "We'll be sworn in as a posse to make sure Smith an' Tranter surrender—"

"But, they won't—"

"Exactly!" Dixon's thin chuckle was sinister as a leveled gun. "Of course they won't! So we'll have tuh shoot 'em out—which'll give us the chance we been lookin' for; we'll blow the whole dang outfit up in smoke!"

Brux licked his lips and shivered.

But an unholy joy lit up Potak's swarthy countenance. Striding to a shelf, he lifted down a bottle and some tin cups. He filled the latter and passed them around. As the others looked at him expectantly, he toasted:

"Here's death tuh Smilin' Smith!" and set his cup down empty.

Dan Hellman sat in the Sheriff's Office at Bucksnort. Elbows on his desk, he sat hunched over, brooding, wondering, scowling. He groaned from time to time and sagged a bit lower in his seat. Deep-etched lines appeared upon his face, lines that had been hardly noticeable before, lines that aged him and gave to his weather-beaten face an air of somber gloom.

Was Smith really the man whom Dixon had seen shoot Bast? Or was Dixon claiming Smith to be the man in the hopes of getting rid of the yellow-haired outlander once and for all?

Why, if Smith was the man, had Dixon insisted that the sheriff send out no warning for other officers to be on the lookout for the boss of the S-Bar-S?

Why did Dixon seem to feel so sure that Smith would be back? Naturally, if Smith had had no hand in the killing of Al Bast, he would be back. But if he *had* killed the Big 3 man, Hellman could conceive of no reason sufficiently urgent to bring him back to what he must know would be a trap.

It seemed, to the puzzled sheriff, that Dixon actually wanted the man to return! Why? How could his return benefit Dixon? Or could it? Or—

A sudden inexplicable chill stole over the sheriff's humped figure as he sat there, elbows resting on his battered desk. He felt a sense of awful helplessness at his inability to pierce the hidden motive he felt sure was back of Dixon's words.

He experienced a feeling of savage desperation as he

wondered if Dixon might not be intending to use the Sheriff's Office for a cat's paw.

There was much about this uneven struggle for Smithers Valley that Dan Hellman could not comprehend. In his heart he felt there must be something more to this than met the eye and ears. On Dixon's part, at any rate. The fellow was deep—deep and deadly.

To be sure, he could appreciate that the syndicate could not afford to lose the range represented by Smithers Valley. It was obvious to any cowman that, without it, the syndicate possessed more cattle than they could feed. Hellman realized, too, that beef prices were pretty much down at the moment, and that if the syndicate were forced to sell their surplus cattle now they would take a staggering loss.

But the thing went deeper, he was sure.

There was another thing that bothered Hellman. Why should Smith have shot Bast? Granted that Bast had attempted Smith's life in the Tall Bottle only that morning. Sill, how could Smith have shot him when he had no gun? Or, had he managed to get one since the sheriff had seen him last?

The more he thought it over, the more the whole affair puzzled the Bucksnort lawman. For two cents, he told himself savagely, he would throw his star in a bog-hole and ride on out of the country!

A bitter laugh twisted the kindly lips beneath the sheriff's ferocious mustache. That was the one thing he could not do. He had to have this job, and he had to keep it—he must somehow manage to be voted in again at the coming election. He had a crippled, parentless niece whose very sustenance was dependent on him, and his continued help was dependent on this job.

After all, he mused sardonically, blood was thicker than water. Smiling Smith would have to look out for himself. He had warned him of it weeks ago.

There was one thing he could do for the outlander; and

even though it estranged him with the syndicate, he meant to do it. He would arrest Smiling Smith the moment that two-fisted outlander returned.

And with this determination, the sheriff put on his hat, turned out the light and locked the office. It was time he hit the hay.

It was getting dusk in the evening of the following day when the Smiler returned to Bucksnort and dismounted from the train. Looking about the town, on his way to the livery stable to get his horse, Smith found things about the same as he had left them. There was but one noticeable difference——the town seemed agitated with the reaction of some exciting happening.

Smiling Smith did not connect the low-muttering groups of townsmen with the incident at the depot the night before. In fact he had just about forgotten Dixon's crazy actions, in the press of his El Paso and Juarez discoveries.

Luckily, it was too dark for him to be recognized from more than a few yards away, and unconsciously, he steered clear of the muttering groups, being in somewhat of a hurry to return to Smithers Valley.

When he reached the livery stable and asked for his flea-bitten nag, Kallis saddled the animal and brought him forth into the yard where Smith stood waiting. Having paid his bill, the Smiler was about to swing into the saddle when a blurred figure strode from the shadows and accosted him.

"That you, Smith?"

"Yeah, but I'm in a hurry, whoever you are, an' ain't got time tuh swap lies now."

"All in a lather tuh git away from town, are yuh?" said the unknown, whose voice seemed strangely familiar. Then the man broke clear of the shadows as he reached Smith's side, where he stood beside his horse. The lantern hung above the stable entrance threw a pale illumination across the speaker's features and Smith recognized the sheriff.

"Howdy, Dan," Smith said. "Yeah, I'm kinda in a hurry tuh make the ranch 'fore bed time. Yuh see, Dolo an' me, we're aimin' tuh git married sometime tomorrow."

"Wal, I reckon you should of got hitched up right after that trouble we had about one of Kallis' hawsses," Hellman said, but not unkindly. "That weddin' of yours will have tuh be put off awhile, I reckon. I hate tuh do it, Smith, but I gotta put yuh under arrest for murderin' Al Bast on the depot platform last night about 8.00 P.M."

Smith's grin disappeared, and his eyes took on a frosty glitter. "What kind of a blazer you tryin' tuh pull, Hellman?"

"It's the Gospel truth, Smith. Jud Dixon swore out a warrant for you last night. He claims he was with Bast when yuh shot him from the train window; says he fired back at you, but yuh ducked below the sill. There's nothin' personal in this, cowboy; I'm jest the Law hereabouts—I gotta do my duty."

As he stood there, between the sheriff and his horse, the hot blood pounded in Smith's head as he comprehended the ghastly situation into which Jud Dixon had manoeuvered him. He had entered a trap, in returning to Bucksnort, and now the trap was about to spring.

Once arrested, who would believe his story? Life imprisonment was the least he could look forward to should he ever come to trial, for the jury would be packed with Big 3 partisans. What then would happen to Dolores?

There was left him but a single alternative—flight. But flight to what, and where? He felt no longing for the Owlhoot Trail. Neither did he fancy the picture that rose before his mind of himself dangling at the end of a lawman's rope!

Dixon had laid his plot with diabolical insight. His clever moves were worthy of admiration, Smith thought, had they not been directed against himself. That Dixon had shot his partner as Bast approached the train, and had then deliberately emptied his weapon at Smith's window would sound like utter nonsense if told before a jury!

The simplicity, the perfect planning and timing of the thing, proved how helpless he was to combat it. The train window was shattered with bullet holes and could be shown in evidence in support of Dixon's story. Smith's possible contention that he'd had no pistol would be laughed to scorn. He'd had ample opportunity to have thrown his gun away.

It took Smith less than three seconds to comprehend the situation, to realize the completeness of this plot against him. Doubtless Dixon had likewise taken measures for his ultimate apprehension should he now escape the sheriff—but it was a chance that he must take. Once in jail his fate would be sealed. Anything seemed better than languishing in one of Bucksnort's stuffy cells to await an inevitabe verdict. Surely nothing could be worse than resignedly submitting to his fate.

The tempestuous surge of the roaring blood passed from his head, leaving him cold, emotionless. His jaw tightened and his eyes grew bleak as, suddenly, his right fist shot forth from his swinging body and caught the sheriff squarely on the chin. Back reeled Hellman beneath that smashing blow. Back and down—spread-eagled in the sand.

As Smith hit the saddle Flea-Bite was throwing dust in a hard run, making for the welcome cloak of night outside the lantern's rays. A streak of flame tore past him as Jed Kallis fired from the hip. Flame spurted from the sheriff's gun as he struggled to his knees.

But the shots went wild as Smith vanished among the murky shadows of the moonless night.

Swiftly the gray's long lunging legs left the county seat behind them, and the twinkling lights of Bucksnort gradually became lost in distance. Smith did not think Hellman would organize a posse to set out on his trail until daylight came to show his tracks. After all, he reasoned, no one would be crazy enough or shrewd enough to think he would be heading for Smithers Valley. Such a course on his part would seem the height of folly.

So Smith spurred on. The desert opened before him like a vast gray blanket.

It was hot and sultry and such vague breezes as sometimes stirred, fanned horse and rider with the heat of flame, searing their skins and parching their throats. And the pungent tang of sagebrush was like a poisonous breath.

It was nearing three when Smith came in sight of the S-Bar-S. The old ranch-house and outbuildings built years ago by Smithers lay huddled in deep shadow. Not a speck of light showed anywhere; it was as though the place was deserted.

As Smith rode into the yard and swung from the saddle before the veranda, a flat voice rasped across the silence from the direction of the bunk-house, a voice that was heavy-laden with menace:

"Halt!"

"It's Smith, Willmoth."

"Yeah? Wal, strike a match an' hold it up to yore face, Smith. We're takin' no chances. Come yuh don't do it afore I count three, I'm lettin' this rifle do the palaverin'."

Hastily Smith scratched a match and, holding it in his cupped hands, turned so that his illumined face was visible from the bunkhouse.

"All right, Smiler," Willmoth called. "C'mon over here. I don't see how in heck you ever got here. We was told by one of them syndicate riders this noon that yuh plugged Bast in town las' night an' pulled out for parts unknowed. We sorta figgered if yuh *had* plugged that ornery sidewinder, yuh'd be havin' all yuh could do a-dodgin' posses."

By this time Tranter had got a lamp lighted. Smith joined them in the bunkhouse and all three sat down on their bunks and looked at one another in silent appraisal.

"Well, buckaroo," sighed Tranter, "how does it feel tuh kill a polecat?"

Smith's lips framed no answering smile. "I ain't never had the pleasure. But I reckon I know one that needs killin' right bad. A two-legged skunk named Dixon."

"Then Bast ain't dead, eh?" Tranter's tone was weighted with regret.

"He's dead, all right, but I didn't have no hand in it," Smith grinned sardonically. "I'm just the fella's rap." He gave his companions a terse account of Dixon's coup, concluding: "I reckon Jud is on the make."

Willmoth nodded gloomily. "Looks like yuh're about tuh be bucked out, Smiler."

Tranter was staring at the light, and there was a far-away look in his faded eyes. Mechanically he produced his battered pipe, whittled a handful of shavings from his plug of Brown Mule, tamped them in the bowl, touched them off by holding the pipe inverted above the lamp and commenced a noisy puffing.

"Let's have the rest of that plug, Buck," Willmoth muttered. "I gotta have somethin' tuh drown that smell."

A painful silence descended.

At last Tranter broke in by saying, "Wal, yuh come here lookin' for a fight, Smiler, an' it begins tuh look right now like it ain't but a short two jumps away. Sometime tomorrow, Dan Hellman will be out here with a posse a-huntin' him a coupla scalps tuh clinch his comin' election. What's she gonna be—run or fight?"

"I dunno. I ain't got much love for owl-hootin' it over the country for the rest of my days. On the other hand, I ain't exactly honin' for a fight. I got the deed to this valley —met Crane in El Paso. But the law in any fight that comes off in this county is gonna be with the Big 3. It it wasn't for Dolo I reckon I'd run. But I can't ask her to marry no durn fugitive."

"So yuh got that pesky deed at last, eh?" Tranter

looked at him thoughtfully. This, he reflected, was not the man he had gone to work for several short weeks ago. This was not the Smith who had lazed around on the ranch-house veranda with him, ready to welcome trouble with widespread arms. This man was different.

This Smith, seated on the bunk across the narrow cabin, was a colder, smoother, far more dangerous hombre than the trouble-hunting youngster to whom he had hired out. This Smith with the cold blue gaze was a man who looked ahead, a man who counted costs. A man from whom all youth's reckless bravado had been purged by the fires of tribulation. A man whom it would be hazardous to cross.

Folding his arms across his chest, Tranter made up his mind to leave all broadcasting of bad news strictly up to Willmoth.

But Willmoth, too, had observed the change in Smith and was almost as loath as the foreman to break the news that must be told.

So they sat with sombre countenances while the silence grew long-drawn; till the air seemed a-quiver with the vibrations of unuttered things.

Gradually the taciturn uneasiness of his men crept in upon Smith's consciousness. His glance was sharp and probing as he looked from one to the other. His pulses began hammering and gray dread rose suddenly in his mind.

"I reckon I ain't heard the worst, yet," he growled. "Well, get it off your chests."

Willmoth shot a furtive look at Tranter, but the foreman's gaze seemed fixed intently on the lamp.

"Mebby it's got somethin' tuh do with Dolo?" Then, as no one seemed to feel it incumbent upon themselves to answer, Smith's tone grew harsh: "Well-"

Willmoth shrugged and wiped the cold sweat from his forehead. "She's gone."

"Gone?" Smith echoed blankly. "Gone where?"

Willmoth looked again at Tranter. "You tell him," the foreman muttered. "I ain't feelin' up to it."

"We don't know—she's jest gone."

"Yuh mean she's left the ranch?"

"We ain't seen her around anywheres since last night."

"What happened last night?"

"Nothin' as we know of—she was readin' a letter when we left the house last night. A letter with a Bucksnort postmark."

Smith started. He remembered the letter he had got from the Post Office and given her. He rememberd kidding her about the Bucksnort townsmen.

Tranter stood up, thrust his hands in his chaps pockets. It looked like a posture of defense.

"Well?" Smith eyed him coldly.

"Umm—" the foreman looked distressed. "We, er, I— I found this down by the stable," he held out a dirty sheet of paper. "It's the letter she was readin'. It was some crumpled up when I found it . . . I," he swallowed painfully—"I reckon yuh can make it out."

Smith took the paper and walked over by the lamp. Spreading it out, smoothing away some of its many wrinkles he made out the penciled scrawl:

> *"Dear Miss:*
> This is tuh let yuh know that yore father was Si Jones, the Bucksnort banker, who used tuh be knowed as Dan Jalnor when he was mayor of El Paso. I got proof of this. He done yore mother dirt. I thot yuh mite like tuh know.
> A FRIEND."

The crumpled missive fluttered from Smith's hand. Tranter's face was before his staring eyes, yet it went unseen. He had never imagined that the log building was so large, that there was such a distance between one bunk-lined wall and the one across from it. It seemed to be growing constantly, to be losing its walls in distance. It made him feel strange, as though he had been deserted in a box-car. The box-car seemed cold, and the chill was biting into him.

"Buck," he said, and the voice seemed that of a stranger, "Buck, get my war sack out from under the bunk. Someplace in it there's a belt an' a pair of guns. Get them for me . . . I've got to think. . . ."

But it was too cold to think. Too cold—

His heart felt like a lump of lead; flexible lead that kept opening and closing. Sometimes it seemed to him that it had gone, so smooth, so easy was its beat. Then without warning it would beat like clanging gongs and galloping fire-horses.

Tranter found his belt and the two bone-handled guns. Mechanically, Smith strapped the dark, brass-studded leather about his lean waist, adjusted the six-shooters in their scarred holsters to confortable positions on his thighs, knotted the thongs about his legs. Then he turned and started for the door, only to stop on a sudden thought.

"Where did you find that letter, Buck?"

"It was on the stable floor, near the stall where we kep' that hawss yuh give her."

"Did yuh try tuh track her this mornin'?"

"It rained last night after she had left," Willmoth grunted.

"Uh-huh," Smith nodded his hard-bitten features expressionless as a sandstone crag. "Well, so long, fellas. I'll be seein' yuh one o' these days."

Tranter sprang forward, grabbed his arm. "Where the heck yuh goin'?"

"I'm headin' for town. It's the most likely place for Dolo tuh go."

"You can't go back there. Don't be a fool! Hellman'll slap yuh in jail!"

"I'm goin'," Smith shook off Tranter's hand. "I've come to appreciate the fact that there can't be a fight without somebody gettin' hurt," he said softly. "We been gettin' the short end of this stick from the start. Things are gonna take a change. Some folks in this country are gonna learn I ain't a right good gent to stack a deck on."

"But you can't lick the whole town!" Tranter snorted.

"I ain't aimin' tuh try, I'm huntin' Dolo."

"But they won't let yuh hunt her," Willmoth objected. "What's more, the minute they spy them guns you're totin' they're gonna grab for their hawglegs an' open up. Yuh got tuh remember, Smiler, it'll be open season on you from here out. Then fellas is gonna try tuh nail yore hide to their fence!"

"Another thing I've learned," Smith's tone was dry, "is that tryin' an' doin' usually ain't quite the same. There's plenty of slips 'twixt the hammer an' the cap." Again he started for the door.

Tranter had scant fear that the hand that had broken up the Wheatleys would prove too slow for the town toughs of Bucksnort, but—

"I'm sort of ridin' townwards tonight myself," he said, and put on his floppy hat. "Got a date with that goldy-headed hash-slinger at the Santy Fe."

"I'll tell her you was detained on account of choliczoo-tic," Smith said.

"Shucks! She won't know what that is!"

"I don't, either—but it's keepin' yuh home." Smith said, firmly, and opened the door.

"Goldy'll give me hell-fire an' brimstone ef I don't keep that date—"

"An' I'll give yuh somethin' worse if yuh do," Smith promised grimly, and closed the door behind him. "Keep your eyes peeled an' your rifles oiled, an' don't let the Big 3 jump this ranch."

Smith stripped his gear from Flea-Bite and turned the animal loose. Shaking out his rope, he strode into the pole-corral. The nervous inmates eyed him warily. They were tall and rangy; he had brought them with him to the Buck-snort country. Some were fuzzy-tails, some bunch-grassers, some hammer-headed and mean of eye. But all had one attribute in common—that quality known to horse-hunters as "bottom."

Gazing about in the light of the low-hung stars, Smith commenced swinging his loop. Suddenly it flew from his hand, went snaking out and snagged the mount of his choice—a long-legged calico paddler.*

In less than no time, he had his saddle on its back and his foot in the stirrup. They struck off down the trail at a ground-eating jog.

Two hours passed during which the desert hush was broken only by the occasional clicking of the calico's shoes against the exposed surfaces of lava outcroppings. Then the Devil's Boot was left behind and they went pounding along in the growing light over the hard-packed surface of a rutted road.

Even yet there was no definite plan of campaign in the Smiler's mind. Such vagrant thoughts as flashed across his numbed mind were still more or less chaotic and unruly. He meant to seek out Dolores. That she was somewhere in the town he had no doubt. He would find her and take her to the ranch, no matter what the cost to himself or others.

It was seven-fifteen by his silver watch when the distant buildings of the town sprang up before him on the plain. Bleached and hard like ancient bones, they looked. But no more grim than the Smiler's smileless countenance as he shook out the reins and increased the calico's pace.

CHAPTER XX

"Yo Te Quiero"

STACKADOLLAH, the gambling manager of the Tall Bottle Saloon & Gambling House, was regarded as something of

* *A pinto that wings out its front feet.*

a mystery by folk living in and around the county-seat of Bucksnort. Where he had hailed from, even the pryingest gossip had been unable fo learn, but it was generally suspected that he had come north from across the Rio Grande on a badly-lathered horse.

He habitually wore the black, funereal garb of a tinhorn gambler, set off by a fancy flower-embroidered vest and a low-crowned flat-brimmed hat. His features were dark, hawk-like and sinister, and if ever a man possessed the evil eye it was this taciturn Stackadollah. His white teeth had never been known to flash in a smile, and his long, lean fingers were well-kept and tapering—the sort of fingers most usually employed with cards or seen curled around the grip of a belching six-gun.

He had a reputation for ice-cold nerve, a reputation enhanced by the four little notches filed in the bone handle of the .45 that swung from his hip in a half-breed holster.

As dawn drew nearer and the crowd in the Tall Bottle diminished to a mere dozen customers, more or less under the weather, Stackadollah crossed to the table near the back of the room where sat Dolores and dropped into an empty chair by her side.

The glance with which he regarded her was not as calm and detached as it had been during the earlier part of the night when she had stood on the little platform by the piano and sang Spanish love songs for the benefit of the patrons. Now there was a smouldering flare in its depths, a calculating light that caused the girl to shiver. Then she thought of that letter, the letter that had driven her in dead of night from the S-Bar-S to this iniquitous den of vice, and a listlessness came over her, an utter indifference to her fate.

"How'd the evenin' go?" the gambler asked in his husky tones. "Not too bad, eh? First night's always the hardest. You'll get used to it. If any of these cow-nurses get too fresh, just give me the high sign—I'll take care of 'em."

"Can I go, now?" she asked. "See, it ees daylight an' I am tired, *señor.*"

"Don't be in a hurry. There's still a good dozen fellas layin' around here lappin' up rot-gut. We can't close till they clear out—or pass out." He cast a look at the fly-speckled clock above the bar. "Gettin' on toward breakfast time, kid. How about eatin' with me, eh?"

Dolores shrugged her slender shoulders. After all, she thought, it made small difference with whom she ate. As well with him as another. The future no longer held rosy visions for her—all was dull and drab ahead. No doubt this hawk-faced gambler would make her as good a man as any other girl with her antecedents might hope to get.

"As you wish, *señor,*" she managed a dreary smile. But her eyes were dull with misery and there were new, tiny lines about her scarlet lips.

He motioned to the bartender and the man brought them a bottle and glasses. Stackadollah poured with a steady hand and a light of anticipation in his evil eyes as he scanned her slender form.

Suddenly her face went white and the color in her cheeks stood out like blotches of paint. Her lips parted as she half rose from her chair, one hand pressed to her breast as though to still the tumult of her pounding heart.

Slowly the gambler turned and looked over his shoulder toward the front of the resort, in the direction the girl was staring.

A man was standing just inside the swinging doors, a tall man who looked about as thin as the proverbial rail. His face, with its long Roman nose and straw-colored close-cropped mustache, was gray and hard like tempered steel. And his eyes were frosty as he sent them about the long room in searching stabs.

The gambler's dark face went taut as he recognized the boss of the S-Bar-S. He got to his feet and pushed back his chair as Smith, having spied the girl, came striding down the long room which had gone so suddenly silent at his appearance.

As Smith came to a pause a scant three feet away, the gambler's eyes grew narrow as he noted the sagging belt with the two filled holsters that circled the Smiler's hips. "Taken to totin' hardware, eh?" he jeered.

But Smith had no eyes for anyone but Dolores. He strode to her side and slipped an arm about her slender waist. "I've come tuh take you home, Dolo," there was a light in his eyes and a tone to his voice that warmed her soul till she remembered that hateful letter. She sagged back in her chair with a sigh.

"I—I have no home but this."

"You belong on the S-Bar-S," Smith said, "an' I've come tuh take you back there."

The girl's cheeks had gone deathly white, and there was a dead, vacant look to her dusky eyes. "You do not understan', *señor*. I—I——" she choked and looked away.

"I know all about that letter. It's a bunch of durned ornery lies! C'mon, let's get out of here——"

"The lady knows what she wants," Stackadollah cut in smoothly, "an' she don't want to go with you."

"Dolo—look at me," Smith said softly. "*Yo te quiero* —I love you. Can't you understand? Even if that vile thing were true, I'd love you just the same. But it isn't! I've seen Don Anastacio—he had your mother's marriage——"

"Listen, you!" Stackadollah's tone was ugly. "I told yuh once the lady ain't interested in yuh. Clear out, an' clear out quick or you'll be carried out on a shutter!"

Still Smith paid no attention to the man. He was gazing at Dolores and her fragile beauty made a dull pounding in his heart.

As if compelled by his hungry glance she rose from her chair and came to him, her wide dusky eyes filled with hope and yearning. Then suddenly she was in his arms and the fragrance of her slender snuggling body mounted to his brain like an exotic perfume. His lips sought hers. . . .

As he released her, a rough hand sent her reeling back against the table and the gambler stood before him, a sneer on his hard thin lips.

"Get your paws off my woman or I'll send yuh out of here horizontal-like!" the tinhorn rasped.

Smith stared at the gambler's white-rimmed mouth and smouldering eyes. Lazily he reached out for the bottle on the table, as though to pour himself a drink. He grasped it about the neck and suddenly his arm flashed forward and the heavy bottle left his hand.

Straight at the gambler's chest it drove.

Stackadollah's black-clad form jerked sideways and the bottle went glinting past. A curse left his lips as his right hand went clawing downward.

Smith's gaunt form dropped into a crouch. Smith's racing palms clutched the handles of his weapons and their hammers rocked beneath his thumbs. Puffs of smoke went swirling upward and the acrid stench of black powder bit at eyes and flaring nostrils. The room went wild with echoes as gun-thunder beat against the silence.

Smith heard a bullet thud against the wall beside him. "Make for the back door!" he growled to the girl. "I'll join yuh in a minute."

Stackadollah was doubled up, clutching at his middle, the gun he had tried to reach forgotten in his pain.

The resort's customers were making for the doors and windows, cursing as they ran. One or two gamblers had appeared from the back room, guns in hand. At sight of Smith, up came their weapons spurting flame. Lead ripped into the wall behind him in a thumping hail of sound.

Again the hammers rocked beneath his thumbs. One of the gamblers spun like a cat reversing ends. But not soon enough. A slug tore through his chest and smashed him to his knees, where he swayed with bloody lips. The second gambler made the door, but collapsed beside it.

Smith felt a jarring impact as a slug tore the heel from his right boot. A second jerked the scarf at his neck, and a third ripped through his vest. He jerked a look along the bar and saw the barkeep with a flaming pistol leveled across its top.

Smith snapped a shot from his left-hand gun and the fellow coughed and disappeared behind his bar.

Confusion was rampant inside the Tall Bottle. The roar of belching guns, the cries and curses of excited men, the shouts and the clumping pound of running feet made a medly of raucous sound that dinned in the throbbing ears of Smiling Smith.

He threw himself abruptly sideways as a shotgun boomed above the tumult. A blast of lead ripped past the spot where he had stood. Cold sweat broke out on his forehead at the narrowness of his escape.

His .45s rocked back against his palms and the shotgun fell from its wielder's hands as the fellow went over backward, hit the floor outsprawled and stayed there.

Swiftly as they had flamed to action a few minutes before the guns went silent and a brooding hush settled over the long room. The rasping sobs of a man in pain came to Smith as he stood there shoving fresh cartridges into the empty chambers of his guns. Yonder, through the drifting powder smoke, he could see a dim form thrashing on the floor.

Alert and ready for hasty action, he went sidling toward the swinging doors of the resort's front entrance. Reaching them, he peered cautiously out above their tops. For a block either way the street seemed clear.

Parting the doors he dashed outside, holstering his guns as he did so. He reached the hitch rail where he had left his calico paddler and, with his left hand, unknotted its reins from the rail. Hastily, then, his eyes played over the other mounts ranged alongside. He must get a mount for Dolores. He saw a bay gelding that looked to have more than the usual speed and slipped its knotted reins.

As he was about to lead the horses into the narrow alley that gave upon the rear of the Tall Bottle, where he had bidden the girl await him, a man plunged out of its mouth and slewed to a halt.

"Smith!" gasped the man, and reached for his gun.

Smith's flushed face, his narrowed steady eyes, did not change expression. But, swinging his whole body behind the arc of his striking fist, he smashed the man beside the ear.

Hat, gun, man and all reeled sideways beneath the force of that lightning jolt, crumpled and struck the ground in a headlong fall. Whirling, Smith sprang to his saddle and, still holding the reins of the second horse in his clenched left fist, went sweeping down the alley.

The girl was waiting. White-faced, she scrambled into the bay's saddle.

"Thank God, *señor,* that you are safe!" she cried, as they went rocketing out across the sage-dotted plain to the road that led toward Smithers Valley.

Smith looked back across his shoulder as they left the town behind. A group of gesticulating mounted men were gathering about the Sheriff's Office. Smith's face darkened as he looked.

"We gotta make it fast, Dolo," he muttered, and jabbed the calico with his spurs.

A half-hour passed and the muffled pound of their horses' hoofs was the only sound to disturb the morning silence. Steadily, mile after mile they rode with the beat of the animals' hearts beneath their knees.

From time to time Smith glanced back across his shoulder, and always he saw the posse, neither gaining nor losing but hanging on tenaciously, holding their fire till a narrowed range should make it immediately effective.

"For why they follow us like that?" Dolores asked once when he looked behind.

"They're after me for the murder of Bast," he said, and her face went white again. "I can't prove it, but it wasn't me that shot him. I didn't take tuh wearin' my guns till las' night."

He flashed her a sidelong look, hardly daring to study her closer.

"Say again what you told me before," she said.

"You—you mean in the Tall Bottle?"

"Si, when you asked me to come back to your *casa grande*."

"*Yo te quiero*—I love you."

"Truly, *señor*?"

"Truly," his voice was a little gruff, as he thought how close he'd come to losing her. "I reckon I ain't very good at this love stuff, Dolo girl. I guess mebbe it's because I ain't never had no experience. I never knew a girl before that I'd care two shucks tuh marry—not till I met you, that is. But you—*yo te quiero!* If we could get hitched up right this minute, it wouldn't be a second too soon!"

Though the posse was spurring hard, and not more than a mile behind them, she sighed with happiness and closed her eyes. "Surely," she whispered, "the *Señor Dios* has heard my prayers."

CHAPTER XXI

Siege!

PAST the sandstone spires and up the green valley the two horses swept, straight up the valley to the broad veranda of the ranch house. There the riders dismounted.

Tranter came striding from the ranch house, a rifle cradled in his arm.

"Shore is good tuh see yuh back, Miz Dolores, ma'am," he said, sweeping off his floppy-brimmed hat. Blushing, Dolores thanked him.

"Where's Willmoth?" Smith spoke brusquely. "If he's around any place, call him."

Tranter put one hand to the side of his mouth and let out a blood-curdling bellow.

Willmoth stepped out the bunkhouse door and leisurely joined them. He, too, Smith saw, carried a rifle in the hollow of his crooked left arm. In these two men, the Smiler realized that he had found treasures. Diamonds in the rough, mayhap, but diamonds, nevertheless. Undoubtedly they were rovers and scoffers at authority, but for his purposes they were far superior to the best tophands in the county.

"Turn all the horses outa the corral," Smith said, "but four. Put the four in the stable for emergencies an' shut the stable door. There's a sheriff's posse not more'n a few miles back. I reckon they stopped at the Big 3 line-camp to strengthen their hand. This has all the earmarks of a showdown, boys. Anyone that ain't feelin' trigger-minded better hop his nag an' light a shuck outa here."

"Listen at him, would yuh," Tranter said to Willmoth. "Thinks he's the only pistol-pusher in these here parts, I shouldn't wonder!"

"Yeah," Willmoth scoffed. "Yuh oughta tell 'im about the time yuh held off the MacCandlas boys for five days an' nights without food or water. That's about the best all-round fracas yuh was ever in, I bet!"

"Fracas?" the shaggy-haired Tranter looked at Willmoth incredulously, "Why, shucks, Trigger, that wa'n't no fracas! Did I ever tell yuh about the time Billy the Kid an' me——"

But Smith cut him off. "Get goin', Willmoth, an' tend tuh them horses—take ours along with yuh. Tranter, you come inside with me. These walls here look like they're solid adobe, all right. I reckon they'll withstand most of the slugs Hellman an' his Big 3 posse will be slammin'. I reckon the ranch house is about the most easily defended structure we got. What's your notion, Buck?"

Tranter shoved his floppy-brimmed hat far back to scratch his head. "I'd say yuh was right. But seems tuh me, a few sacks o' flour piled alongside some of them front winders might sorta come in handy. Should they open up with highpowered rifles, some o' their slugs might take tuh leakin' in, I shouldn't wonder."

As Tranter followed the girl inside, Smith stared thoughtfully at the heavy walls and massive front door with its strengthening bands of hammered iron at top and bottom. A most appropriate door for a time like this, he thought grimly. Old Smithers had built his home to last and Smith, its present owner, was mighty thankful that he had. This giant door would stand a deal of battering. Oak, it was, and eight feet high and a good six inches thick!

As he rejoined Tranter inside, the latter got out his battered old pipe and began whittling fodder for it from his ever-handy plug. "About what time," he asked, "do yuh reckon that posse is due tuh open the festivities, Smiler?"

"Hard tellin', Buck. May be headin' this way right now. Then again, they may be waitin' for night. Be kinda hard for 'em to find good shelter round here in the daytime, so I sorta incline toward the notion they'll wait for dark."

"That'd be my guess, too. I notice yuh ain't doin' an over-amount of grinnin' this afternoon, Smiler. What's wrong? The prospect of settlin' this business fer once an' fer all oughta cheer yuh up, I should think. Besides, if we win, that case ag'in' yuh that Brother Dixon framed will be all shot tuh pieces."

"You don't expect us tuh win, I hope," Smiler snorted. "All I'm figgerin' on is mebbe gettin' 'em to come to terms. The way it is, things are in a awful mess. But if I show Sheriff Hellman my deed for this place, that will spike one of the syndicate guns, mebbe———"

"Yeah, an' mebbe not! If we don't win this here ruction, Smiler, you're gonna be headed fer hell on a down-hill grade, an' no mistake! If yuh stand trial fer Bast's killin', yuh'll be good as convicted afore the jury's even picked!"

"I know it," Smith nodded, and his face was grim. "But it's hard, bitter hard, tuh realize there ain't no way of endin' this business by anything except hot lead. Did yuh ever stop tuh think, Buck, that by this time tomorrow night, we may all be planted? Dolo an' me was aimin' to get hitched up tomorrow."

Tranter scowled. "Yore trouble, young fella, can be spelled in one word. You got that epidemic what the sky-pilots refer to as 'religion'." He shook his head lugubriously. "Don't try tuh tell me different. I had it once myself—it was right after that time my third wife run off with that travelin' soap salesman from Frisco."

After a cold supper eaten in the dark behind barricaded doors and windows, the defenders of the Smithers place sat for the most part in gloomy silence. There was not much to look forward to. If they lost, the best they could hope for was to be taken to jail. And from the jail, they held little doubt but that Smith and Tranter at least would be conducted to the gallows. Willmoth as an accessory, might get off with a long prison term. What would happen to Dolores was a matter of conjecture.

If they won, Smith could not see that they would fare much better. They would be outlaws and constantly hunted from hole to hole until at last their careers should be inevitably ended by hot lead. Neither prospect was at all alluring.

"You reckon, Smith, that the Big 3 are after yore scalp account of your settlin' on range what they've used so dang long they got no intention of givin' it up?" Willmoth broke the silence.

Smiler nodded, with one arm clasped tight around Dolores' slender waist. Then realizing that the other man could not see him, he answered: "Yeah."

"Well, don't never think it. That Dixon's got a head on him, an' he ain't riskin' it fer no penny-ante game like free grass. I ain't no mind-reader, but I can tell yuh that there's a heap more to it than that. Gosh, yes! Didn't yuh never hear of the fella what built this here rancho? Old Smithers, he was called."

"Yeah, I've heard of Smithers," Smith replied, indifferently. "A bad 'un from all accounts. One of them 'stand an' deliver' gents what used tuh work the Santa Fe Trail, wasn't he?"

"Yuh guessed it—he shore was. Ended his career at the end of a twelve-foot rope," Willmoth assured his audience. "The story goes that after robbin' the Wells Fargo Company of a big gold shipment from the El Dorado Mine, Old Smithers busted up his gang an' cached his gold ingots an' such somewheres around this ranch. The Big 3 been usin' this spread for several years, an' every year Jud Dixon used tuh spend most of his time pokin' around here lookin' for that hidden treasure. Bast used tuh give him the hawss-laff frequent, but he kept right on a-huntin'."

"From what I've heard," said Tranter, "that there treasure's well worth huntin'. Gold bars alone are worth a fortune! Thirty of 'em! Half an inch thick, three inches across an' ten inches long! Cripes, yuh can't blame Jud fer wantin' tuh get his hands on them!"

For a full minute there was silence. Then Smith said astounded: "Whew! Gee-willickers!"

The next instant all thoughts of gold had fled the minds of the four crouched by the windows of the darkened ranch house.

"Sh-!" Tranter hissed.

Came then to straining ears the sound of galloping hoofs pounding the hard packed earth. Like thunder it was, so loud and awesome did it come rolling across the midnight hush.

Soundlessly each man sped to his chosen position beneath the opened windows. All but Smith, who was already crouched by his, with Dolores at his side. In vain had he tried to get her to leave him for a place of comparative safety. Her place, she claimed, was by his side, and there she stayed, deaf to his pleading and threats.

Cold rifle-butts cuddled eager shoulders as the men crouched beside their windows; six-guns, oiled and ready, hung loose in their holsters.

A shrill whistle abruptly blared through the night and stilled the pounding hoofs.

All lights had long been extinguished in the ranch-house. In the inky darkness that obtained within, Smith crouched beside that window closest to the massive front door. Tranter held a position commanding the left portion of the yard—that giving on the distant bunkhouse. Willmoth covered the side facing the stable.

There was little or no danger from the rear. A deep crevice with glass-smooth sides made a charge from that direction impossible.

High up in the purple sky a full moon was hopping merrily from cloud to scudding cloud, as though unaware of the grim battle about to be enacted on the range below. Yet, Tranter, peering up at it from his place beside an aperture, remarked in his customary sardonic way:

"Wal, fellas, looks like there'll be blood on the moon 'fore mornin'."

"Yeah," grunted Willmoth, "an' two or three gents in unknowed graves!"

It was well after twelve when Sheriff Hellman and his posse, reinforced by the gun-slingers from the Big 3 approached in single file the hollow wherein sat the ranch buildings of the S-Bar-S.

In the shadow-dappled moonlight, the darkened buildings lay wrapt in a slumberous hush. To the posse's alert eyes there came no slightest movement to animate the peaceful scene—no movement, that is, save that created by the low wind among the cottonwoods. Yet Hellman and Dixon felt positive that behind those distant, darkened windows lay grim defenders, alert and ready.

The sheriff blew a loud blast on his whistle and the

posse deployed, spread out in a silent circle, rifles ready in their hands.

For some moments Hellman studied the ranch house, a dark blur amid the shifting shadows. Then, hauling a large white handkerchief from his coat pocket, he tied it to his rifle-barrel and rode slowly forward into the open. When he had approached within fifty feet of the defenders' position, a harsh voice rasped:

"Halt!"

The sheriff checked his horse and sat there waiting.

"What is it, Hellman?" came Smith's voice.

"I've got warrants for you an' Tranter," the lawman's grim voice gave evidence that he had not forgotten the un-expected blow Smith had dished him out the previous evening. "You're wanted for the murder of Bast, an' Tranter's wanted on a rustling charge. I'd advise you men to surrender immediately and without any demonstration of violence."

"An' I'd advise you, yuh weak-kneed coyote," growled Tranter, "tuh git outa range as fast as yuh can travel if yuh value yore hide!"

"Are yuh surrenderin' peacefully, Smith?" demanded Hellman, harshly.

"No."

"I'm warnin' yuh; I've got eye-witnesses to you an' Tranter an' Willmoth havin' set afire the headquarters ranch of the Big 3 syndicate, to you having personally murdered Bast in cold blood, an' to Tranter havin' rustled Big 3 stock."

Smith's cold chuckle rang across the moonlit silence. "Must be more eye-witnesses on the Big 3 payroll than punchers!" he jeered.

Hellman turned his horse without a parting word and rejoined his posse.

Hardly had he done so than one of his men sent a shot thudding into the adobe ranch house. Instantly spurts of flame blossomed in the darkened windows. Lead whined above the possemen's heads as they scrambled from their saddles. Oaths and shots rang out and were muffled in the roaring blast of belching guns.

One of the posse clutched his shoulder and went reeling from the saddle he had not deserted swiftly enough; went down beneath the churning hoofs of his terrified mount. Further to the left a squealing horse reared upright and the moonlight flashed from its steel-shod hoofs.

Inside the adobe ranch house Smith and his companions hugged the walls as guns roared out in a mad staccato, pouring their streams of thudding lead at the earthen walls. And through the chatter and cough of barking rifles, the deep bass voice of a buffalo gun boomed sullenly from time to time.

With wild, blood-curdling yells, the syndicate men with their brother possemen from the county seat came rushing toward the house. Some ran recklessly toward open windows. Others, more cautious, dashed for the ranch house door, that massive oaken barrier.

Up went wild, baffled, high-pitched yells of rage as they found the barrier unyielding, saw the windows as sheets of orange flame. And above and through their shouts and oaths roared the vicious crash of gunfire, like a pagan anthem to their song of death.

"Rush that door, you fools!" roared Dixon's husky voice. "Shoot out the lock!"

"Don't be a bigger jughead than yuh are," snarled the syndicate foreman. "It ain't got a lock! Yuh orta know there's two eight-inch bars of oak holdin' it from the inside."

"That's so," Dixon muttered. "Get a log some place some of you fellas. We gotta bust that dang thing down!"

"Try it an' see how much it costs!" Tranter bawled, belligerently.

Smith squatted in a half-crouch beside his window, Dolores at his side, one arm across his shoulders. Both his six-guns were in his hands, his heart was pounding, his spine crawling as he waited for the searing impact of hot lead to go ploughing through his body.

Across the yard the dim forms of crouching men could be seen advancing through the fog of powder smoke, jets of lurid flame spurting from the leveled weapons in their hands.

But flame, too, still blossomed from the windows of the ranch house. Leaving her lover's side, Dolores ducked about from window to window reloading the defenders' empty pistols from the piles of cartridges beneath each guarded opening.

Again the posse was charging, aiding their comrades by a withering blast of lead to bring their battering log against the great front door. Thrice they had tried the side, but too many windows made the kitchen door as impregnable as a fortress.

Smith saw Monahan, suddenly, among the charging line. And the following instant saw him drop his gun and whirl to flee, only to spin dizzily and fall prone upon his face.

Another outlaw clutched his middle suddenly as Smith rocked a shot through the glassless opening before him. A man to the fellow's left staggered back with a lurid curse that was lost in the thunder of belching guns.

Panic-stricken, the outnumbering possemen broke and scattered, racing for the shelter of the distant cottonwoods that framed the clearing.

Through a back window, unguarded because of the gully behind the house, climbed several syndicate men, more wily than their less-imaginative fellows. They held ready pistols in their hands and meant to use them if opportunity offered.

Silently and suddenly from the inky shadows a tall gaunt figure leaped among them. Each of his hands held a gun, and each gun was being swung with silent fury. Beneath the awful gun-whipping administered by his skillful hands, men reeled and slumped and dared not shoot for fear of hitting one of their own number in their place of murky shadows. Groans and curses filled the air.

"You was askin' for it, gents!" Smith gritted. "An' now you're gonna get it!"

The front sights of his glinting weapons were leaving a trail of havoc in their swinging wake, tearing, maiming, cracking. With howls for mercy, shooting wildly in their sudden panic, the syndicate holster-hoppers, as Tranter called them, clambered through the window in frantic haste to get again beneath the star-filled sky. All but two; these unfortunates had been shot by their companions in their desperate efforts to down the pistol-whipping Smith.

Having dispersed this faction admirably, the Smiler raced to the front of the house again to join Dolores and his men. Things at the front, he found, were not going so nicely now. The two windows facing the front commanded a fair portion of the yard outside. But they were wholly inadequate for covering the door, due to the thickness of the adobe walls.

Even as he returned to his former position, covered by the belching guns of the again-advancing posse, Potak, Brux and several of their men were driving a heavy log with telling effect against that oaken door. On the instant, Smith realized that even such a massive barrier as this could not withstand such pressure long.

"Willmoth! Tranter!" his voice was grim and hard. "Help me get them chairs an' that table an' that buffet moved away from the door. We gotta get 'em back a ways an' build a breastwork. An' we gotta work durn fast; that door won't hold up long. Bring some of them sacks of flour away from the window ledges, too!"

In the gun-rocked silence the three men worked like mad, and presently Smith muttered: "Whew! That'll do, boys. Get your rifles loaded now so's we can give Jud Dixon's friends a hot reception that won't be forgotten in a hurry. When the door goes down, open up an' give them polecats all yuh got!"

Yet hardly were the words out of his mouth when, with a splintering crash of rending wood and broken hinges, the great oaken barrier was hurled to the floor. From behind their hastily constructed breastworks the three defenders, aided by the moon's bright rays, poured a withering blast of lead into the surging huddle of men that filled the cavity.

Smith saw as in a dream Tranter's rifle recoil against his shoulder as its muzzle vomited lead and flame. By the gun flashes he could see the wolf-like grin on Willmoth's twisted lips, and the wrinkle-edged squint of his puckery gray eyes as he sighted down the barrel of his thundering Sharps. These men were fighting for their lives just as he was fighting for his own; quarter was a thing unthought of, indeed unknown, to these long-riders of the range.

The attempt of the posse to breach the house's adobe walls was shattered at its very moment of triumph. The posse broke in headlong fright as man after man reeled and staggered, stumbled and gasped and fell in that moon-bathed doorway. It was as though Ol' Man Death himself stood there with swinging, dripping scythe and a ghastly grin on his bony lips.

Smith dropped his heated rifle and sprang forward past the breastworks, making for the yard. Tranter and Willmoth followed cat-footed, unquestioning, at his back, their hands on their holstered belt-guns.

CHAPTER XXII

SUNRISE IN SMITHERS' VALLEY

ACROSS the broken door they scrambled, and over fallen bodies purchased by a greedy syndicate for forty-a-month-and-found. Smith strode determinedly out of the murky shadows, leading the way into the brightness of the open yard. And in his heart dwelt an expectation of sudden death, and a great fear that he had gazed for the last time upon the fragile beauty of Dolores' piquant face.

But though there was fear in his heart, his stride never faltered, his clenched jaw never slacked.

Enough good men had died tonight, more than enough red blood had quenched the thirst of New Mexico's sandy soil. No matter what the cost to himself, Smith was determined to stop this ghastly butchery if he could.

Straight into the open Smith led the way and stopped. Tall and straight and cold, he stood there in the argent light. And if the faces of his companions were grim and powder-streaked and set, Smith's saturnine visage was more so.

They were taking an awful chance, coming out in the open this way. All three of them knew it, but only Smith knew why they were here.

As he faced the clearing with its hidden syndicate gunmen, Smith's mouth was a tight-lipped line beneath his scrubby, yellow mustache. It was a brave thing he was doing, a rare gesture to save bloodshed and further death. He expected death to be his portion, yet he paused and raised his hand:

"If any of you gents out there don't know me," he said clearly, "no doubt you've heard of the fella that's squatted on the Smithers place an' is accused of killin' Bast. I'm him—Smilin' Smith from Painted Stick," he paused.

Yet, strangely, the posse withheld its fire. Perhaps they were awed by the very audacity of his move. The daredevil three could hear the hoarse cursing of Jud Dixon as they stood there. Then, abruptly, Smith went on:

"I didn't want this fight; I tried my durndest to persuade the Big 3 that nothin' was gonna drive me from this ranch. But they wouldn't have it that way. I reckon you gents can all see what's come of their plottin' an' schemin'——" his outflung hand indicated the huddled shapes in the moon-bathed doorway at his back.

"Gents, if I'm promised fair treatment, I'm willin' to stand trial for the killin' of Al Bast, though I didn't have anything to do with it. But I ain't aimin' tuh go to trial with a jury box packed with Big 3 partisans. If you gents don't like to leave here with some of your friends unavenged, why that's up to you; but we'll fight tuh the last damn gasp if yuh force our hands!"

"We got enough," growled Brux from the shadows. "Smith's right. It's been our crowd that's prodded him right along. Jud Dixon, especial. I'm sick of this shootin' an' killin'. Sheriff, take charge of this affair."

"Why, you yeller-livered pup!" came Dixon's snarling voice. "I'd like tuh get my hands around yore skinny neck for about five minutes!"

Then the sheriff's voice rang across the clearing. "You S.Bar-S fellas drop your guns an' we'll come down there an' palaver. This business has got to be talked over."

"Mebbe so, but I ain't throwin' down my gun fer nobody!" Tranter snorted. "I got a heap too much respect fer my neck!"

"Yeah, we're keepin' our guns," Smith said.

Slowly the riders of the syndicate followed the town members of the posse into the clearing before the adobe ranch house, the moonlight showing their slitted eyes aglitter beneath the brims of their Stetson hats. The Sheriff and Jud Dixon fronted the possemen, Brux having warily circled to the side where Smith and his two men stood. Dolores, too, had joined them.

There were, Smith saw when he looked around, but four syndicate men aside from Brux and Dixon present. Where the others had gone to was a matter for conjecture, though Smith believed that the men not actually killed had decided to depart forthwith for a less hazardous climate than that around the Bucksnort range.

"Wal," Dan Hellman said to Smith, "I reckon it's up tuh you to start the conversation."

"No, it ain't," Brux broke in nervously. "It ain't up to Smith at all, Sheriff. Jud Dixon's the one that ought to explain things. He planned 'em an' he oughta pay for 'em. He's a danged murderin' hound!"

"What's that?" Hellman looked as though he could hardly believe his ears.

Smith shot a covert glance toward where Dixon, a bloody bandage around his left leg, was supported by one of his men. There was fear and murderous hate in the man's bright-button eyes as he glared at his partner.

"Don't pay no attention to that yeller-bellied rat, sheriff. He's tryin' tuh squeal himself out of a tight hole," Dixon sneered malignantly.

"Mebbe I am," Brux quavered, "but I don't aim tuh take punishment for somethin' I had no hand in. You an' Bast cooked up all this deviltry against Smith so's tuh scare him outa Smithers Valley. An' it's my guess yuh murdered Si Jones, hopin' tuh palm it off on Smith! Yuh wasn't home that night till long after the fire at headquarters, an' when you got there, yore horse was pretty near jiggered, yuh'd run him so hard. What was yore hurry if yuh wasn't tryin' to ride yoreself an alibi?"

"Why, you slat-sided wart!" Dixon's low tone was venomous. "You tell another lie like that an' I'll wring your skinny neck!"

"Brux is right, Sheriff," Smith broke in. "Let him talk! I know for almost certain that Dixon killed Bast so he could frame me. I believe Brux is tellin' gospel truth."

Hellman glanced to one another of them dubiously. "Well, go on, Brux," he said at last. "I ain't heard you talk so much since I've known yuh."

"I'm tellin' the truth as I know it," Brux muttered doggedly, and in the moonlight his face looked pale and drawn. "I ain't tryin' to lie outa anythin'—I'm jest tryin' tuh see that Justice grabs itself the right man. *An' that man is Jud Dixon!* He must have murdered Si Jones because the next day I saw him lookin' over some of the papers that Jones allus kept locked up in that safe in his private office!"

"That's a dang lie," Dixon's voice was hoarse. "A dirty, rotten lie!"

"It ain't no lie, an' you know it!" Brux snarled. "What's more, I don't believe the S.Bar-S had anythin' tuh do with that fire we had—that was probably started by some careless puncher with a cigarette. There was a terrible wind blowin' that night. Anyhow, even if Smith was mixed up in that fire, I don't blame him. Dixon had Bast and some of the men derail three carloads of Smith's sheep at Big Bend trestle a few weeks ago. If Smith set that fire, he wasn't doin' nothin' more than gettin' even!"

"I didn't tell Bast to derail those sheep, you little rat!" Jud Dixon bellowed.

"No?" Brux grinned. "Well, I bet you killed Bast and Jones. I saw yuh shoot Potak in the back tonight durin' the fight, an' you know it! Yuh tried tuh pot me, too, but I jumped jest in time," he patted his bandaged arm significantly, and grimaced at the pain. "What's more, I ain't the only one that saw yuh down Potak! Lefty Flynn saw yuh do that, an' Lefty's here tuh prove it!"

"Uh-huh!" Flynn affirmed, stepping forward. "I saw him—"

Dixon, cornered, laughed. But his hard-chiseled face was chalky and his eyes were wells of burning hate. "Take this, you yeller-bellied squealers!" he suddenly snarled through twisted lips, and his right hand went flashing down and up in a single blurring movement. Red flame spouted from his hip.

Brux tried to save himself, to fling himself aside—but too late! Wild yells of fright from the surrounding punchers mingled with his choking screams as he went down with two bullets in his chest. Curses and shouts rang through the clearing, while for several red moments all was turmoil and confusion. Yet over all came the steady *crack-crack-*

crack! of Dixon's belching weapon.

Flynn clutched at his middle and went over on his face. A man beside Smith staggered backward cursing. Smith grabbed for his guns, but there was no longer any need.

For several seconds Tranter had been watching Jud Dixon closely. When his hand had streaked for his gun Tranter had been watching. But he saw no sense in keeping Brux alive. He watched unmoved as Dixon's shots cut the squealer down.

But as Dixon's gun began its swing toward Smith, Tranter burst into action like a coiled spring abruptly released. His hand seemed to procure a gun by magic, and in the same instant it went off. Just once—but once was quite enough.

A ludicrous expression of surprise came over Dixon's hard-chiseled features, and his mouth dropped open and hung that way. Then a convulsive tremor shook his body and he pitched forward in the dust. He did not move again.

Half an hour later, after the sheriff had shaken hands with Smith and gone, and the syndicate men had departed with their grisly burdens, Dolores and Smith, followed by Tranter and Willmoth, re-entered the bullet-scarred ranch house. Smith and the girl paused while Tranter struck a match and hunted up some candles. All the chimneys for the coal-oil lamps had been demolished during the fight. But Tranter found some candles and ignited their wicks. With their golden mellow light softening the harsh marks of conflict, the four friends glanced round.

Abruptly Willmoth started, stared, stretched forth a shaking hand: "Look! By the front door! By the everlastin'! Criminy-gee! jest *look* at that! Gold in bars! *Piles of 'em!*"

Smith and Dolores stared at the broken door and the golden bars peeping through the wreckage incredulously. Surely it could not be real, they thought. It seemed impossible that there could be that much gold in the world!

But sight of such treasure did not provoke undue emotion in Tranter. He bestowed but a slighting look upon it, wrinkled his nose and scoffed: "Prancin' prairie chickens! that ain't nothin' but the Wells Fargo loot that ol' Smithers hooked back in '89. Cripes! did I ever tell you folks about the time I discovered that gold mountin' over in——?"

"Never mind thinkin' up any more o' them whoppers," Willmoth interrupted. "I can't listen an' look at the same time, an' right now I'd rather look. See there, Smiler? That ol' door was holler. No wonder she caved in s' quick. You'll be rich as Creases!"

"Shucks," Smith said, unruffled. "Any fella would be rich if he had Dolo," and his arm tightened around the slim, willowy form of the dusky-eyed girl at his side. "Dolo is the sweetest gal in the whole Southwest—bar none!

"You fellas have stuck by me through thick an' thin, through fair weather an' foul, an' it's only fittin' that yuh share my luck. From here on out, boys, we share an' share alike—in the gold, in the ranch, an' in anythin' else that may come our way.

"There's jest one thing I won't share with yuh, pardners, an' that's Dolo. She an' me aim to go forkin' a coupla broncs to Bucksnort on urgent business jest as soon as you fellas can slap a pair of saddles on two of them nags in the stable. We'll be back sometime this evenin' an' you two gents can have the pleasure of steppin' right up an' sayin' 'Howdy' to Mrs. Smilin' Smith!"

★★★★★★★★★★★★★★★★★

The Biggest, Boldest, Fastest-Selling Titles in Western Adventure!

★★★★★★★★★★★★★★★★★

CHARTER'S MOST WANTED LIST

Elmer Kelton
_ 15266-X DONOVAN $2.50
_ 76066-X SHADOW OF A STAR $2.50
_ 80447-0 THE TEXAS RIFLES $2.50

Frank Bonham
_ 07876-1 BREAK FOR THE BORDER $2.50
_ 77596-1 SOUND OF GUNFIRE $2.50

Giles A. Lutz
_ 34286-8 THE HONYOCKER $2.50
_ 88852-6 THE WILD QUARRY $2.50

Will C. Knott
_ 29758-7 THE GOLDEN MOUNTAIN $2.25
_ 71146-6 RED SKIES OVER WYOMING $2.25

Prices may be slightly higher in Canada.

Available at your local bookstore or return this form to:

 CHARTER
Book Mailing Service
P.O. Box 690, Rockville Centre, NY 11571

Please send me the titles checked above. I enclose _____ Include 75¢ for postage and handling if one book is ordered; 25¢ per book for two or more not to exceed $1.75. California, Illinois, New York and Tennessee residents please add sales tax.

NAME _____

ADDRESS _____

CITY _____ STATE/ZIP _____

(Allow six weeks for delivery.)   **431**